Rolf Boldre~~

The Crooked Stick

Rolf Boldrewood

The Crooked Stick

1st Edition | ISBN: 978-3-75232-684-0

Place of Publication: Frankfurt am Main, Germany

Year of Publication: 2020

Outlook Verlag GmbH, Germany.

THE CROOKED STICK

BY ROLF BOLDREWOOD

CHAPTER I

The time, the close of a lurid sultry February day, towards the end of a long, dry summer succeeding a rainless winter, in the arid region of West Logan. A blood-red sun sinking all too slowly, yet angrily, into a crimson ocean; suddenly disappearing, as if in despotic defiance of all future rainfall. A fiery portent receding into the inferno of a vast conflagration, was the image chiefly presented to the dwellers in that pastoral desert, long heartsick with hope deferred.

The scene, a limitless stretch of plain—its wearisome monotony feebly broken by belts of timber or an infrequent pine-ridge. The earth adust. A hopeless, steel-blue sky. The atmosphere stagnated, breezeless. The forest tribes all dumb. The Wannonbah mail-coach toiling over the furrows of a sandhill, walled in by a pine thicket.

'Thank God! the sun is down at last; we must sight Hyland's within the hour,' exclaimed the passenger on the box-seat, a tall, handsome man, with 'formerly in the army' legibly impressed on form and feature. 'How glad I shall be to see the river; and what a luxury a swim will be!'

'Been as hot a day as ever I know'd, Captain,' affirmed the sun-bronzed driver, with slow decision; 'but'—and here he double-thonged the off-wheeler, as if in accentuation of his statement—'heat, and flies, and muskeeters, dust and sand and bad water, ain't the wust of this road—not by a long chalk!'

'What the deuce *can* be worse?' demanded the ex-militaire, with pardonable acerbity. 'Surely no ruffians have taken to the bush lately in this part of the world?'

'Well, I did hear accidental-like as "The Doctor" and two other cross chaps, whose names I won't say, had laid it out to stick us up to-day. They'd heard that Mr. Tracknell was going up to Orange, and they have it in for him along o' the last Bandamah cattle racket.'

'Stop the coach, the infernal scoundrels! What do they expect to do next? The country won't be fit for decent people to live in if this sort of thing is not put a stop to.'

'Well, Captain Devereux,' replied the driver, a tall, sinewy, slow-speaking son of the soil, 'if I was you I wouldn't trouble my head about them no more than I could help. It ain't your business, as one might say, if they've a down on Tracknell. He nearly got the Doctor shopped over them Bandamah cattle, an' he wasn't in it at all, only them Clarkson boys. My notion is that Tracknell got wind of it yesterday, and forgot to come a purpose.'

'So, if a gang of rascally cattle-stealers choose to stop the coach that I travel in, I am to sit still because I'm not the man they want, who did his duty in hunting them down.'

'Now hear reason, Captain! There ain't a chap in the district, square or cross, that would touch you, or any one from Corindah—no, not from here to Baringun. The place has got such a name for being liberal-like to gentle and simple. If we meet those chaps—and we've got the Wild Horse plain to cross yet—you take my tip and say nothing to them if they don't interfere with you.'

The man to whom he spoke raised his head and gazed full in the speaker's face. The expression of his features had changed, and there was a hard set look, altogether different from his usually frank and familiar air, as he said, 'Are you aware that I've held Her Majesty's commission?'

The driver took his horses in hand, and sent them along at a pace to which for many miles they had been strangers, as they left the heavy sand of the pine-hill and entered upon the baked red soil of the plain.

'I'm dashed sorry to hear it now,' he said slowly. 'Some people's mighty fond of having their own way. Yes, by God! I was afeared they'd block us there. They're a-waiting ahead near that sheep break—three of 'em. That's the Doctor on the grey. Blast him!'

With this conclusively fervent adjuration, Mr. Joe Bates pulled his horses into a steady yet fast trot, and approached the three men, who sat quietly on their horses near a rough timber fence which, originally constructed for counting a passing flock of sheep, partly obstructed the road.

Captain Devereux looked keenly at the strangers, then at the driver, as he drew forth a revolver of the latest pattern.

'Listen to me, Bates! I can make fair shooting with this at fifty yards. When they call on you to stop, draw up the team quietly but keep them in hand. Directly I fire, send your horses along. It is a chance if they offer to follow.'

'For God's sake, Captain, don't be rash,' said the young fellow earnestly. 'I'm no coward, but remember there's others on the coach. Once them chaps sees Tracknell ain't a passenger, they'll clear—take my word. You can't do no good by fighting three armed men.'

'Do as you're told, my good fellow,' returned his passenger, who seemed transformed into quite another personage from the good-natured, easy-going

3

gentleman with whom he had been chatting all day, 'unless you wish me to believe that you are in league with robbers and murderers.'

Joe Bates made no further remonstrance, but drew the reins carefully through his hands in the method affected by American stage-coach drivers, as he steadily approached the spot where the men sat, statue-like, on their horses. As the coach came abreast of them the man on the grey turned towards it, and, with a raised revolver in his hand, shouted, 'Bail up!'

The leaders stopped obedient to the rein. As they did so Captain Devereux fired three shots in rapid succession. The first apparently took effect on the rider of the grey horse, whose right arm fell to his side the instant after he had discharged his pistol. The second man staggered in his seat, and the horse of the third robber reared and fell over on his rider, who narrowly escaped being crushed. At the same moment, at a shout from the driver, the team started at a gallop, and taking the road across the plain, hardly relaxed their speed until the hotel at the angle of the Mackenzie River was in sight.

Looking back, they caught one glimpse of their quondam foes. Two were evidently wounded, while the third man was reduced to the grade of a foot-soldier. There was, therefore, no great probability of pursuit by this highly irregular cavalry force.

'By George! Captain,' said the driver, touching up the leaders with renewed confidence as he saw the outline of the roadside inn define itself more clearly in the late twilight, 'you can shoot straight and no mistake. Dashed if I could hit a haystack without a rest. The Doctor and one of the other chaps fired the very minute you did. One ball must have gone very close to you or me. I felt pretty ticklish, you bet! for I've seen the beggar hit a half-crown at twenty yards before now.'

'I believe he *did* hit me,' said Devereux, coolly putting his hand to his side. 'It's only a graze; but we'll see when we get down. I scarcely felt it at the time.'

'Good God!' said the kind-hearted young fellow. 'You don't say so, Captain? There's blood on your coat too. We'll have a look as soon as we get to Hyland's.'

'It's a strange thing though,' continued Devereux, 'that unless you're hard hit you never know whether a gunshot wound is serious or not. It's not my first knock, and I certainly shouldn't like it to be the last, after an engagement of this nature. However, we shall soon see.'

Something was in the air. As they drew up before the inn door, the customary group awaiting one of the great events of bush life was noticeably swelled. A

4

confused murmur of voices arose, in tones more earnest than ordinary events called forth. The driver threw his reins to a helper, and took the landlord aside.

'We've been stuck up, and there's been a bit of a brush with the Doctor's mob. They've got it hot, but the Captain's hit too. You send a boy to Dr. Chalmers at Hastings township, and that darkie of yours to the police station. The Captain had better get to bed. The mails are right and the passengers.'

The hotelkeeper, beyond a brief and comprehensive dedication of the false physician to the infernal powers, forebore remark, and so addressed himself to the practical alternative, that within five minutes two eager youngsters, one black and one white, were riding for their lives towards the points indicated, brimful of excitement not altogether of an unpleasant nature, as being the bearers of tragical tidings, and thus to be held free from blame—indeed, to be commended—if they did the distance in less than the best recorded time.

Inside the hotel the bustle was considerable. The bar was crowded, groups of men surrounded the inside passengers, who had each his tale of wonder and miraculous escape to relate. 'The Captain had behaved like a hero. Knocked over one man, broke the Doctor's shoulder, and dropped the third chap's horse nearly atop of him. If there'd only been another revolver in the coach they'd have took the lot easy. All the same, they'd just as well have let them have what they'd a mind too. They only wanted to serve out Tracknell, and when they found he wasn't there they'd have gone off as like as not. If the Captain was hurt—as looked likely—his life was worth all the bushrangers between here and Bourke, and a d——d bad swop at that.'

'Well, but some one must fight,' said a pot-valorous bar loafer, 'else they'd take the country from us.'

'That's a dashed sight more than *you*'d do, in my opinion,' retorted the speaker, who was a back-block storekeeper. 'We can do our share, I suppose, when there's no other show. But we should have been all safe here now if we'd taken 'em easy—a few notes poorer, but what's that? The police are paid for shooting these chaps, not us. And if the Captain never goes back to Corindah, but has to see it out in a bush pub like this, I say it's hard lines. However, Chalmers will be here in an hour—if he's sober—and then we'll know.'

The sound of galloping hoofs in less than the specified time caused every one to adjourn to the verandah, when the question of identity, as two figures emerged from a cloud of dust, was quickly settled by a local expert. 'That's the doc's chestnut by the way he holds his head, and he's as sober as a judge.'

'How can you tell that?' queried a wondering passenger.

5

'Why, easy enough. Doc.'s not man enough for the chestnut except when he's right off it. When he's betwixt and between like he takes the old bay mare. She stops for him if he tumbles off, and would carry him home unsensible, I b'leeve, a'most, if she could only histe him into the saddle.'

The medical practitioner referred to rode proudly into the inn yard unconscious of the critical ordeal he had undergone, and throwing down the reins of his clever hackney, walked into the house, followed by the respectful crowd.

'Bad affair, Hyland,' he said to the landlord. 'Which room? No. 3? All right! I'll call for you as soon as I look the Captain over. It may be nothing after all.'

Entering the bedroom to which the wounded man had retired, he found him sitting at a small table, smoking a cigar with his coat off and busily engaged in writing a letter. This occupation he relinquished, leaving the unfinished sheet and greeting the medico cordially. 'Glad to see you, doctor. Wish it was a pleasanter occasion. We shall soon know how to class the interview— Devereux slightly, seriously, or dangerously wounded has been in more than one butcher's bill. One may hold these things too cheap, however.'

'Take off your shirt, Captain; we're losing time,' said the doctor; 'talk as much as you like afterwards. Hum! ha! gunshot wound—small orifice—upper ribs—may have lodged in muscles of the shoulders. Excuse me.' Here he introduced a flexible shining piece of steel, with which he cautiously followed the track of the bullet. His brow became contracted and his face betrayed disappointment as he drew back the probe and wiped it meditatively in restoring it to its case. 'Can't find the bullet—gone another direction. Take a respiration, Captain. Good. Now cough, if you please.'

'Do you feel any internal sensation; slight pain here, for instance?' The Captain nodded affirmatively. 'Inclination to expectorate?'

'Yes.'

'Ha! much as I feared. Now put on your shirt again; and if I were you, I'd get into bed.'

'Not just yet, if you'll allow me; we had better settle this question first. Is the matter serious—you know what I mean—or only so so?'

'You're a strong man, Captain, and have seen all this before. I shall tell you exactly how the matter stands. This confounded lead pill, small as it is, has not taken the line I hoped it had towards the shoulder or lumbar muscles. It has turned inwards. You have been shot through the lungs, Captain, and, of course, you know the chances are against you.'

The wounded man nodded his head, and lit another cigar, offering the doctor one, which he took.

'Well! a man must go when his time comes. All soldiers know that. For my wife's sake and the darling of our hearts' I could have wished it otherwise. Poor Mary! It might have been avoided, as the driver said; but then I should have had to have changed natures with some one else. It is Kismet, as the Moslem says—written in the book of fate from the beginning of the world. And now, doctor, when will the inflammation come on?'

'Perhaps to-night late; certainly to-morrow.'

'I may smoke, I suppose; and I want to write a letter before my head gets affected.'

'Do anything you like, my dear sir. You can't catch cold this weather. Take a glass of brandy if you feel faint. No, thanks! none for me at present. See you early to-morrow. I'll tell Mrs. Hyland what to do if hæmorrhage sets in. Good-night!'

The doomed man smoked his cigar out as he gazed across the broad reach of the river, on a high bluff of which the house had been built. 'Done out of my swim, too,' he muttered, with a half smile. 'I can hardly believe it all to be true. How often a man reads of this sort of thing, little expecting it will come home to himself. Forty-eight hours, at the utmost, to prepare! How the stars glitter in the still water! To think that I shall know so much more about them before Saturday, most probably at any rate. What a strange idea! Poor Mary! what will she do when she hears? Poor darling! expecting me home on Saturday evening, and now never to meet on earth. Never, nevermore! To think that I kissed her and the bright, loving little darling Pollie—how she clung round my neck!—for the last time! The last time! It is hard, very hard! I feel a choking sort of feeling in my chest—that wasn't there before. I had better begin my letter. The letter—the last on earth.'

He flung away the fragment of the cigar, and sat down wearily to the letter which was to be the farewell message of Brian Devereux to his wife and child. How dear they were to him—reckless in some respects as his life had been—until then, he never knew before. He sat there writing and making memoranda until long after midnight. Then he lit one last cigar, which he smoked slowly and calmly to the end. 'They are very good. I may never get another. Who knows what the morrow may bring forth? Good-night, my darlings!' he said, waving his hand in the direction of Corindah. 'Good-night, sweet fond wife and child of my love! God keep and preserve you when I am gone! Good-night, my pleasant home, its easy duties and measureless content! Good-night, O earth and sea, wherein I have roamed so far and sailed so many a league! Once more, darlings of my heart, farewell! A long good-night!'

And so, having an instinctive feeling that the hour was at hand when the injured mechanism of the fleshly frame, grandly perfect as it had hitherto proved itself, would no longer provide expression for the free spirit, Brian Devereux, outworn and faint, sought the couch from which he was never to arise. At daylight he was delirious, while the frequent passage of blood and froth from his unconscious lips confirmed the correctness of the medical diagnosis. Before the evening of the following day the proud, loyal, gallant spirit of Brian Devereux was at rest. He lies beneath the waving desert acacia, in the graveyard by the river allotted to the little town of Hastings. He was followed to the grave by every man of note and position in a large pastoral district; and on the marble tombstone which was in the after-time erected at the public cost above his mortal remains are included the words:—

'SACRED TO THE MEMORY OF BRIAN DEVEREUX,
LATE CAPTAIN OF H.M. 88TH REGIMENT,
WHO WAS MORTALLY WOUNDED BY BUSHRANGERS
WHILE MAKING A GALLANT AND SUCCESSFUL DEFENCE.
HONOUR TO THE BRAVE!'

So fell a gallant man-at-arms, obscurely slain—ingloriously in a sense, yet dying in strict accordance with the principles which had actuated him through life. There was deep, if not ostentatious, sorrow in his old regiment, and more than one comrade emptied his glass at the mess table more frequently the night the news came of the death of Brian Devereux, whom all men admired, and many women had loved.

Brave to recklessness, talented, grandly handsome, the darling of the mess, the idol of the regiment, the descendant of a Norman family long domiciled in the west of Ireland, he had always exhibited, commingled with brilliant and estimable qualities, a certain wayward impatience of restraint which at critical periods of his career had hindered his chance of promotion. A good-natured superior, on more than one occasion, had reported favourably on differences of opinion scarcely in accordance with the canons of the Horse Guards. At length a breach of discipline occurred too serious to be overlooked. In truth, a provoking, unreasonable martinet narrowly escaped personal discomfiture. Captain Devereux was compelled to send in his papers, to the despair of the subalterns and the deep though suppressed discontent of the regiment.

Sorely hurt and aggrieved, though far too proud for outward sign, he resolved to quit the mother-land for the more free, untrammelled life of a new world.

The occasion was fortunate. The sale of his commission, with a younger son's portion, sufficed at that time to purchase Corindah at a low price, on favourable terms. Adopting, with all the enthusiasm of his nature, the free, adventurous career of an Australian squatter, he married the fair and trusting daughter of a high Government official—herself a descendant of one of the old colonial families of distinction,—and bade fair, in the enjoyment of unclouded domestic happiness and the management of a confessedly improving property, to become one of the leading pastoral magnates of the land.

But who shall appease Fate? The bolt fell, leaving the fair, fond wife a widow, and the baby daughter fatherless, whose infantine charms had aroused the deepest feelings of his nature.

After the first transports of her grief, Mrs. Devereux, with the calm decision of purpose which marked her character, adopted the course which was to guide her future life. At Corindah she had tasted the early joys of her bridal period. There her babe had been born. There had her beloved, her idolised husband—the worshipped hero of the outwardly calm but intensely impassioned Mary Cavendish—pleased himself in a congenial occupation, with visions of prosperity and distinction yet to come. She would never leave Corindah. It should be her home and that of his child after her. Her resolution formed, she proceeded to put in practice her ideas. She retained the overseer —a steady, experienced man, in whom her husband had had confidence. She went over the books and accounts, thus satisfying herself of the solvency and exact position of the estate. This done, she explained to him that she intended to retain the establishment in her own hands, and trusted, with his assistance, to make it progressive and remunerative.

'Captain Devereux, my poor husband,' she said, 'had the greatest confidence in you. It is my intention to live here—in this place which he loved and improved so much—as long as there is sufficient for me and my baby to live on. I shall trust to you, Mr. Gateward, to do for me exactly as you would have done for him.' Here the steady voice trembled, and the tears that would not be suppressed flowed fast.

'I will do that and more, Mrs. Devereux,' said the plain, blunt bushman. 'Corindah is the best station on the river, and if the seasons hold middling fair, it will keep double the stock it has on now in a few years. You leave it to me, ma'am; I'll be bound the run will find a home and a snug bank account for you and missie for many a year to come.'

Between Mr. Gateward and Corindah Plains, 'the best run on this side of Mingadee,' as the men said, the promise had been kept. The years had been favourable on the average. When the dire distress of drought came there had been a reserve of pasture which had sufficed to tide over the season of adversity. Besides this, Corindah was decidedly a 'lucky run,' a favoured 'bit of country.' When all the land was sore stricken with grass and water famines, it had springs which never ran dry; 'storms' too fell above Corindah; also strayed waterspouts, while all around was dry as Gideon's fleece. In the two decades which were coming to an end when Pollie Devereux had reached womanhood, the rigid economy and unwavering prudence with which the property had been managed had borne fruit. The credit balance at the bank had swelled noticeably during the later and more fortunate years. And Mrs. Devereux was known to be one of the wealthiest pastoral proprietors in a district where the extensive run-holders were gradually accumulating immense freeholds and colossal fortunes. A temporary check had taken place during the last most unfortunate season. No rain had fallen for nearly a year. The loss of stock on all sides had been terrific, well-nigh unprecedented. Mrs. Devereux, rather over-prudent and averse to expenditure (as are women mostly, from Queen Elizabeth downwards, when they have the uncontrolled management of affairs), had felt keenly the drawbacks and disasters of the period.

'I wonder if we shall get our letters to-morrow, mother,' said Pollie Devereux to that lady, as they sat at breakfast at Corindah on one clear, bright autumnal morning. 'Things do really happen if you wait long enough.'

'What is going to happen?' asked the elder lady dreamily, as if hardly aroused from a previous train of disturbing thoughts. 'We are all going to be ruined, or nearly so, if the winter proves dry. Mr. Gateward says the cattle never looked so wretched for years, and the poor sheep are beginning to die already.'

'Mr. Gateward is a raven for croaking; not that I ever saw one, but it sounds well,' replied the girl. 'He has no imagination. Why didn't he send the sheep away to the mountains before they got so weak, as Mr. Charteris and Mr. Atherstone did? It will be all his fault if they die, besides the shocking cruelty of slow starvation.'

'He is a conscientious, hard-working, worthy man,' said Mrs. Devereux. 'We should find it difficult to replace him. Besides, travelling sheep is most expensive. You are too impatient, my dear. We may have rain yet, you know.'

'I wish I had been a boy, mother,' replied the unconvinced damsel, drumming her fingers on the table as she looked wistfully through the open casement, festooned by a great trailing climber, to where the dim blue of a distant mountain range broke the monotony of the plain. 'It seems to me that none of the men we know have energy or enterprise enough to go beyond the dull round of routine in which they have been reared. Sheep and cattle, cattle and sheep, with a little turf talk for variation. They smoke all day, because they can't talk, and never think. Surely new countries were not discovered or the world's battles fought by people like those I see. I think I should have been different, mother, don't you?'

'I am sure of that, my darling,' answered the mother with a sigh, patting the girl's bright abundant hair as she rose in her eagerness and stood before her. 'You put me in mind of your father when you look like that. But you must never forget that the world's exciting work is rarely allotted to women. The laws of society are harsh, but those of our sex that resist them are chiefly unhappy, always worsted in the end. My girl cannot help her eager, impatient heart, but she will never despise her mother's teaching, will she?'

'Never while life lasts,' said the girl impetuously, throwing her arm round the elder woman's neck, and burying her face in her bosom with childlike abandon—'not when she has an angel for a mother, like me; but I *am* so tired and wearied out with the terrible sameness of the life we lead. Though I have been here all my life, I seem to get less and less able to bear it. I am afraid I am very wicked, mother, but surely God never intended us to live and die at Corindah?'

'But you will be patient, darling?' said the mother tenderly, as with every fond endearment she soothed the restless, unfamiliar spirit newly arisen from the hitherto unruffled depths of the maiden's nature. 'You know I had intended to take you to Sydney for the summer months, if this terrible season had not set in. But when——'

'When the rain comes, when the grass grows—when the millennium of the pastoral world arrives—we may hope to have a glimpse of Paradise, as represented by Sydney, the Botanical Gardens, and the Queen's-birthday ball. That's what you were going to say, mother darling, wasn't it? Poor old mother! while you're fretting about those troublesome sheep, poor things, that always seem to be wanting water, or grass, or rock-salt, which doesn't happen to be procurable—here's your ungrateful, rebellious child crying for the moon, to make matters worse. I'm ashamed of myself; I deserve to be whipped and sent to bed—not that I ever was, you soft-hearted old mammy. Besides, isn't this delightful unknown cousin, Captain Devereux, coming some fine day? He's a whole chapter of romance in himself. I declare I had forgotten all about him.'

The foregoing conversation was held in the morning room of the very comfortable cottage—or one might say *one* of the cottages—which, with a score of other buildings of various sorts and sizes, heights and breadths, ages and orders of architecture, went to make up Corindah head station. Perhaps the building referred to had the highest pretension to be called 'the house'—inasmuch as it was larger, more ornate, and more closely environed with

11

flower-beds, shrubs, and trailing, many-coloured climbers, all of which bore tokens of careful tendance—than any of the others. As for the outward appearance of the edifice, it was composed of solid sawn timber, disposed outwardly in the form of horizontal slabs, lined more carefully as to the inner side; the whole finished with gay, fresh wall-papers and appropriate mouldings. A broad, low verandah ran around the house. A wide hall, of which both back and front doors seemed to be permanently open, completely bisected the building. Wire stands, upon which stood delicate pot-plants of every shade of leaf and flower, gave a greenhouse air to this division. At a short distance, and situated within the enclosed garden, was a smaller, older building of much the same form and proportion. This was known as 'the barrack,' and was delivered over to Mr. Gateward and such bachelor guests as might from time to time visit the station. This arrangement, which often obtains in bush residences, is found to be highly convenient and satisfactory. In the sitting-room smoking and desultory, even jovial conversation can be carried on, together with the moderate consumption of refreshments, around the fire, after the ladies of the household have retired, without disturbing any one. In summer the verandah, littered with cane lounges and hammocks, can be similarly used. In the event of an early departure being necessary, the man-cook of the junior establishment can be relied on to provide breakfast at any reasonable, or indeed unreasonable, hour.

On several accounts Corindah was looked upon as a representative station, one of the show places of the district. It was a stage which was seldom missed by any of the younger squatters who could find a convenient excuse for calling there, upon the journey either to or from the metropolis. It was a large, prosperous, naturally favoured tract of country, a considerable and increasingly valuable property. It was managed after a liberal, hospitable, and kindly fashion. Mrs. Devereux, though most unobtrusive in all her ways, permitted it to be known that she did not approve of her friends passing the door without calling; and they were, certainly, treated so well that there was no great inducement to neglect that form of respect. There was yet another reason why few of the travellers along the north-western road, friends, acquaintances, or even strangers, passed by the hospitable gate of Corindah. During these eventful years Mary Augusta, generally spoken of as 'Pollie Devereux' by all who could claim anything bordering upon the necessary grade of intimacy, had grown to be the handsomest girl within a hundred miles of the secluded spot in which she had been born and brought up.

And she was certainly a maiden fair, of mien and face that would have entranced that sculptor of old whose half-divine impress upon the marble will outlast how many a changing fashion, how many a fleeting age! Tall, lithe, and vigorous, yet completed as to hand and foot with an exquisite delicacy that contrasted finely with the full moulding of her tapering arms, her stately poise, her rounded form, blue-eyed, tawny-haired, with classic features and a regal air, she looked like some virgin goddess of the olden mythology, a wood-nymph strayed from Arcadian forests ere earlier faiths grew dim and ancient monarchs were discrowned.

CHAPTER II

The heiress of Corindah had been carefully educated in a manner befitting her birth, as also the position she was likely to occupy in after-life. Governesses had been secured for her of the highest qualifications, at the most liberal salaries. Her talents for music and drawing had been highly cultivated. For the last three years of her educational term she had resided in Sydney with a relative, so that she might have the benefit of masters and professors. She had profited largely by instruction. She had read more widely and methodically than most young women. Well grounded in French and Italian, she had a handy smattering of German, such as would enable her, in days to come, either to perfect herself in the language by conversation or to dive more deeply into the literature than in the carelessness of youth she thought necessary.

These things being matters of general knowledge and common report in the district, it was held as a proved fact by the wives and daughters of her neighbours that Pollie Devereux had got everything in the world that she could possibly wish for. Agreed also that, if anything, she was a great deal too well off, having been petted and indulged in every way since her babyhood. That she ought to be only too thankful for these rare advantages, whereas at times she was discontented with her lot in life, and professed her desire for change—which was a clear indication that she was spoiled by overindulgence, and did not know what was for her real good. That her mother, poor Mrs. Devereux, ought to have been more strict with her. These well-intentioned critics were not so far astray on general principles. They, however, omitted consideration of one well-established fact, that amid the hosts of ordinary human beings, evolved generation after generation from but slightly differing progenitors, and amenable chiefly to similar social laws, strongly marked varieties of the race have from time to time arisen. These phenomenal personages have differed from their compeers in a ratio of divergence altogether incomprehensible to the ordinary intelligence.

Whence originating, the fact remains that each generation of mankind is liable to be enriched or confounded by the apparition of individuals of abnormal force, beauty, or intellect. Neither does it seem possible for the Attila or the Tamerlane, the Semiramis or the Cleopatra of the period to escape the destiny that accompanies the birthright, whether it be empire or martyrdom, the sovereignty of hearts or the disposal of kingdoms. In spite of all apparent restraint of circumstance, the unchangeable type, dormant perhaps for centuries, reasserts its ancestral attributes.

Such,

> 'Till the sun turns cold,
> And the stars grow old,
> And the leaves of the Judgment-book unfold,'

will be the course of Nature. The 'mute inglorious Milton' is the poet's fiction. He is not mute, but bursts into song, which, if a wild untutored melody, has the richness of the warbling bird, the power of the storm, the grandeur of heaven's own wind-harp. The 'Cromwell guiltless of his country's blood' remains not in the stern world of facts the patient hind, the brow-beaten servitor. He leads armies and sways nations. To the soldier of fortune, who smiles only on the battlefield, and comprehends intuitively the movements of battalions, book-knowledge is superfluous and learning vain. He finds his opportunity, or makes it. And the world of his day knows him for its master.

And the queen of society, what of her? Like the poet, *nascitur non fit*, she is born not manufactured. Doubtless, the jewel may be heightened by the setting, but the diamond glitters star-like in the rough. The red gold-fire burns in the darksome mine. Pollie Devereux, her admirers asserted, would have ruled her *monde* had she been born a nursery-maid or an orange-girl. Her beauty, her grace, her courage, her natural *savoir-faire*, would have carried her high up the giddy heights of social ladders in despite of all the drawbacks which ever delayed the triumph of a heroine.

Still, the while we are indulging in these flights of imagination, our bush-bred maiden is a calmly correct damsel, outwardly conventionally arrayed, and but for a deep-seated vein of latent ambition and an occasional fire-flash of brilliant unlikeness, undistinguishable from the *demoiselles bien-élevées* of eighteen or twenty that are to work such weal or woe with unsuspicious mankind. In a general way this young woman's unrest and disapproval of her environments merely took the form of a settled determination to explore the wondrous capitals, the brilliant societies, the glory and splendour of the Old World—to roam through that fairy-land of which from her very childhood she had eagerly read the legends, dreamed the dreams, and learned the languages. 'Eager-hearted as a boy,' all-womanly as she was in her chief attributes, she could not slake the thirst for change, travel, and adventure, even danger, with a draught less deep than actual experience. If she had been her father's son instead of his daughter, the inborn feeling could hardly have been stronger.

When she thought of leaving her mother, in whom all the softer feelings of her heart found their natural home and refuge, she wept long and often. But still the passionate desire to be a part of all of which she had read and dreamed, to see with her eyes, to hear with her ears, the sights and sounds of far lands, grew with her growth and strengthened with her strength. As the months, the years rolled on, it acquired the power of fate, of a resistless destiny for good or evil; of a dread, unknown, controlling power, which beckoned her with a shadowy hand, and exercised a mysterious fascination.

That there are men so formed, so endowed with natures apart from the common herd of toilers and pleasure-seekers, no one doubts. It is equally true that there are women set apart by original birthright as clearly distinct from the tame tribes of conventional captives. But society, to strengthen its despotic rule, chooses to ignore the fact, preferring rather to coerce rebellion than to decorate distinction.

The eventful days leading slowly, but all too surely, towards the tragedy which is too apt to follow the idyllic course of our early years, fleeted by; a too peaceful, undisturbed period had arrived. Another morning broke clear and bright, as free from cloud or wind, mist or storm wrack, in that land of too changeless summer, as if winter had been banished to another hemisphere.

'Oh dear!' exclaimed Pollie, as springing from her bed she ran lightly to the open window, and drawing up the green jalousies gazed wistfully at the red golden shield of the day-god slowly uprearing its wondrous splendour above the pearl-hued sky-line, while far and near the great plain-ocean lay in dim repose, soundless, unmarked by motion or shadow. 'Ah me, how tired I am of the sight of the sun! Will it never rain again? How long are we to endure this endless calm? this bright, dismal, destructive weather? I never realised how cruel the sun could be before. As a child I was so fond of him, too, the king of light and warmth, of joy and gladness. But that is only in green-grass countries. Here he is a pitiless tyrant. How I should delight in Europe to be sure, with ever-changing cloud and mist, even storm! I am aweary, aweary. I have half a mind to ride out and meet the coach at Pine Ridge—I feel too impatient to sit in the house all day. What a time I have been standing here talking or thinking all this nonsense! I wish I could help thinking sometimes, but I *can't* if I try ever so hard. Mother says I ought to employ myself more; so I do, till I feel half dead sometimes. Then I get a lazy fit, and the thinking, and restlessness, and discontent come back as bad as ever. Heigho! I suppose I must go and dress now. There's no fear of catching cold at any rate. Now I wonder if Wanderer was brought in from Myall Creek?'

Acting upon this sensible resolution, and apparently much interested in the momentous question of her favourite hackney having been driven in from a distant enclosure, failure of which would have doomed her to inaction, Pollie's light form might have been seen threading the garden paths; after which she even ventured as far as the great range of stabling near the corner of the other farm buildings. Here she encountered the overseer, Mr. Gateward,

16

when, holding up the skirts of her dress so as to avoid contact with the somewhat miscellaneous dust which lay deeply over the enclosure, she thus addressed him—

'Good-morning, Mr. Gateward! Do you think it will ever rain again? Never mind answering that question. Russell himself knows no more than we do, I believe. What I *really* want to know is, did they bring Wanderer in from the Myall Creek? because I *must* ride him to-day.'

'Yes, Miss Pollie, the old horse came in. I told them not to leave him behind on any account. There's no knowing what may happen in a dry year. Very well he looks too, considering. You'll find him in his box. We'll soon have him fit enough. He's worth feeding if ever a horse was, though chaff's as dear as white sugar.'

'I should think he was, the dear old fellow. I knew you'd look after him, and I wasn't mistaken, was I? I can always depend on you.'

'You'll never want a horse, or anything else you fancy, Miss Pollie, while I'm on Corindah,' said the veteran bushman, looking tenderly at the girl. 'What a little thing you was, too, when I first know'd you; and what a grand girl you've grow'd into! I hope you'll be as happy as you deserve. You've a many friends, but none of 'em all will do more for you than poor old Joe Gateward, 'cept it might be Mr. Atherstone. That's what I'd like to see, miss——'

'Never mind Mr. Atherstone; you're all so good to me,' said the girl, blushing, as she took the hard, brown hand in hers and pressed it warmly in her slender palm. 'I feel quite wicked whenever I feel discontented. I *ought* to be the happiest girl in Australia. Perhaps I shall be when I'm older and wiser. And now I must run in. I want to put fresh flowers on the breakfast-table; but I must first go and say good-morning to dear old Wanderer.'

She dashed off to the loose box, and opening the door, gazed with sparkling eyes at the good horse that stood there munching his morning meal of chaff and maize with an appetite sharpened by weeks of abstinence from anything more appetising than extremely dry grass and attenuated salt-bush.

'Oh, you darling old pet!' she cried, as she walked up to his shoulder, passing her taper fingers over his velvety face and smooth neck, silken-skinned and delicate of touch even after the trials of so hard a season. 'And your dear old legs look as clean as ever! Was it starved and ill-treated in that nasty bare paddock? Never mind, there's a load of corn come up. I know who'll have his share now, however the rest may come off. Now go on with your breakfast, sir, for I must get mine, and we'll have a lovely gallop after lunch.'

The grand old hackney, nearly thorough-bred, and showing high caste in every point, looked at the speaker with his mild, intelligent eyes, and then waving his head to and fro, as was his wont when at all excited, betook himself once more to his corn.

The day wore on slowly, wearily, with a dragging, halting march, as it seemed to the impatient maiden. The sun rose high in the hard blue sky, and glared, as was his wont, upon the limitless pastures, dry and adust, the pale-hued, melancholy copses, the fast-falling river, the forgotten creeks. The birds were silent; even the flies held truce in the darkened rooms—there was a deathlike absence of sound or motion. Hot, breezeless, unutterably lifeless, and for all less vigorous natures relaxing and depressing, was the atmosphere. To this girl, however, had come by inheritance, under the mysterious laws of heredity, a type of quenchless energy, a form combining the old Greek attributes of graceful strength and divinely dowered intellect, impervious alike, as were her anti-types, to sun and shade, to fatigue or privation, to climatic influence or untoward circumstance.

'Mother,' she said, after tossing about from sofa to chair, from carpet to footstool, the while the elder woman sat patiently sewing as if the family fortunes depended upon the due adjustment of

Seam and gusset and band,
Band and gusset and seam,

'I must go and put on my riding-habit. I shall die here, I'm certain, if I stay indoors much longer. I feel apoplexy coming on, or heart disease, I'm sure. Besides, there is a breeze always outside, or we can make one, Wanderer and I, on the plain.'

'My darling, it's surely too hot to go out yet,' pleaded the mother.

'It's twice as hot indoors,' retorted the wilful damsel, rising. 'I'll ride as far as the Mogil Mogil clump; you can send little Tarpot after me as soon as he gets the cows in. But a gallop I must have.'

The sun was declining as the girl rode out of the paddock gates, but no hint of coolness had as yet betokened the coming eve. The homestead was still and solitary of aspect, as a Mexican hacienda at the hour of the siesta, but for a different reason. Hot and wearisome as had been the day, every man about the place had been hard at work in his own proper department, and had been so occupied since sunrise.

In Australia, however scorching the day, how apparently endless and desolating the summer, no man, being of British birth or extraction, thinks of intermitting his daily work from sunrise to nightfall, except during the ordinary hours allotted to meals.

So the overseer was away on his never-ending round of inspection of stock —'out on the run,' as the phrase is—to return at, or perhaps long after, nightfall. The boundary riders were each and all on their different beats— some at the wells; others at the now treacherous and daily more dangerous quagmires surrounding the watering-places, from which it was their duty to extricate the feeble sheep. No one was at home but a small native boy named Tarpot, with whose assistance Pollie managed to saddle her loved steed. Leaving injunctions with him to follow her as soon as he should have brought up the cows, she turned her horse's head to the broad plain; and as he snuffed up the fresh dry air and bounded forward in a stretching gallop along the level sandy track, the heart of the rider swelled within her, and she wished it was not unfeminine to shout aloud like the boy stock-riders who occasionally favoured the musters of Corindah with their company.

The well-bred animal which she rode was fully inclined to sympathise with his mistress's exhilaration. Tossing his head and opening his nostrils, Wanderer dashed forward along the far-stretching level road, just sufficiently yielding to be the most perfect track a free horse could tread at speed, as if he were anxious to run a race with the fabled coursers of that sun now slowly trailing blood-red banners and purple raiment towards his western couch. Mile after mile was passed in a species of ecstatic eagerness, which for steed and rider seemed to know no abatement. The homestead faded far behind them, and still nothing met the view but the endless grey plain; the mirage-encircled lines of slender woodland opening out north and south, each the exact counterpart of the other. An ever-widening, apparently illimitable waste, a slowly retreating sun, a sky hopeless in unchanging, pitiless splendour of hue, looking down upon a despairing world of dying creatures.

'The Mogil Mogil clump is a short ten miles,' she said, as she reined her impatient steed and compelled him to walk. 'I mustn't send along the poor old fellow so fast; he's not quite in form yet. I shall be there before the coach passes, and then have plenty of time to ride home in the cool. What a blessed relief this is from that choking atmosphere indoors!'

Another half-hour and the clump is reached. Still no sign of the stage-coach visible, as it should be for a mile or two, even more on that billiard table of a plain. The girl's impatient spirit chafed at the unlooked for delay. As she gazed upon the red sun, the far-seen crimson streamers, the endless, voiceless plain, the spirit of rebellion was again roused within her. She sat upon her horse and looked wistfully, wearily over the arid drought-stricken levels. She marked the sand pillars, whirling and eddying in the distance. They seemed to her fanciful imagination the embodied spirits of the waste—the evil genii of the Eastern tale, which might at any time, unfolding, disclose an Afreet or a Ghoul. The thought of long years to be spent amid these vast solitudes seemed to her hateful—doubly unendurable. Before her rose in imagination the dull familiar round of all too well known duties, occupations, tasks, and pleasures, or but feeble, pulseless alternations from the mill-horse track which people call duty.

'Was I born only for such a fate?' she passionately exclaimed. 'Is it possible that the great Creator of all things, the Lord and Giver of Life, made this complex, eager nature of mine to wear itself out with aimless automatic movements, or frantic struggles against the prison bars of fate? Oh! had my father not been cut off in his prime, in what a different position we should have been! We could have afforded to travel in Europe, to revel in the glories of art, science, and literature, to look upon the theatres of the great deeds of mankind—to *live*, in a word. We do not live in Corindah—we grow.'

Overcome by the emotions which the enthusiasm of her nature had suffered temporarily to overwhelm her ordinary intelligence, she had not noticed that the stage-coach, bringing its bi-weekly freight of letters, newspapers, and passengers, had approached the clump of wild orange trees, on the edge of which she had reined her steed. The sensitive thorough-bred, more alive to transitory impressions than his mistress, aroused by a sudden crack of the driver's whip, started, and as she drew the curb-rein, reared.

'What a naughty Wanderer!' she exclaimed, as, slackening her rein, she leaned a little forward, stroking her horse's glossy neck, and soothing him with practised address. At the same moment the four-horse team swept past the spot, and revealed the unwonted apparition to the gaze of the passengers, male and female, who, from the fixed attention they appeared to bestow upon her, were much interested in the situation. Apparently the young lady was not equally gratified, inasmuch as she turned her horse's head towards the distant line of timber which marked the line of the homestead, and swept across the plain like the daughter of a sheikh of the Nejd.

'What a handsome girl!' said a passenger on the box-seat; 'deuced fine horse too—good across country, I should say. Not a bushranger, I suppose, driver? They don't get themselves up like that, eh?'

'That's Miss Devereux of Corindah,' answered the driver, in a hushed, respectful accent, as who should say to the irreverent querist in Britain, 'That's the squire's daughter.' 'She came up here to see if the coach was coming; we're past our time, nearly half an hour. Got thinking, I suppose, and didn't know we was so close. I cracked my whip just to let her know like.'

'But suppose her horse had thrown her,' asked the inquiring stranger, 'what then?'

'Beggin' your pardon, sir, there's mighty few horses that can do that—not in these parts anyway. She can ride anything that you can lift her on; and she's as kind-hearted and well respected a young lady as ever touched bridle-rein.'

Now ever since Corindah had been 'taken up' in the good old days when occupation with stock and the payment of £10 per annum as license fee were the only obligatory conditions encumbering the sovereign right to use, say, half a million acres of pastoral land, the adjoining 'run' of Maroobil and its proprietors had been associated in men's minds among the floating population of the district.

Both had been 'taken up,' or legally occupied, the same year. The homesteads were at no great distance from each other, so placed with the view to being mutually handy in case of a sudden call to arms when the blacks were 'bad.' More than once on either side the 'fiery cross' had been sent forth, when every available horse and man, gun and pistol, of the summoned station had been furnished.

Old Mr. Atherstone, a Border Englishman, had died soon after Brian Devereux, leaving his son Harold, then a grave boy of twelve, precociously wise and practical as to the management of stock, and a great favourite with Pollie, then a tiny fairy of three years old, who used to throw up her hands and shout for joy when Harold's pony came galloping up to the garden gate. He had watched the child grow into a tall slip of a girl, with masses of bright hair, never very neatly braided. He had seen the unformed girl ripen into a beautiful maiden, an enchanting mixture to his eye of much of the old daring, wilful nature mingled with a sweet womanly consciousness inexpressibly attractive. He could hardly recollect the time when he had not been in love with Pollie Devereux. And now, in these latter years, he told himself that there was but one woman in the world for him—nor could it ever be otherwise.

Men varied much in their dispositions. He knew that by observation and experience. There was Bob Liverstone, whose heart (as he himself repeatedly averred) was broken beyond recovery, his prospects of happiness eternally ruined, his life blasted, because of the beautiful Miss Wharton, with her pale face, raven hair, and haunting eyes, who wouldn't have him. He broke his heart over again shamelessly within six months, after unsuccessful devotion to a blonde with eyes like blue china; and finally married a lady who bore not the least resemblance in mind, body, or estate to either of her predecessors being plump, and merely pretty, but exceptionally well dowered.

These and similar divagations of the ardent male adult Harold had seen—seen with alarm and surprise primarily, then with amused assent. For himself he could as little conceive such oscillations in his own tastes and affections as he could fancy himself emulating the somersaults of an acrobat or the witticisms of a clown. No! thrice no! For a man of his deep, dreamy, passionate, perhaps originally melancholy, nature there was but one sequel possible after the deliberate choice of youth had been ratified by the calm reason of manhood. If fate denied him this happiness, all too perfect for this world—the unearthly, unutterable bliss which her love would confer—there should be no counterfeit presentment, no mocking travesty of the heart's lost illusions. He had rightly judged that as yet the girl's feeling for him was that of a pure and deep friendship, but of friendship only. The love of a sister, unselfish, sinless, seraphic, not the fiercer passion akin to hate, despair, revenge in its inverted forces, bearing along with it the choicest fruits that mortal hands can cull, yet joined in unholy joy, in perverted triumph to the groans of the eternally lost, to the endless torment, the dread despair of the prison vaults beneath.

Thus Harold Atherstone watched and waited—awaited the perhaps fortunate turn of events, the effect of the moral suasion which he knew Mrs. Devereux gently exercised. And she had told him that he was the one man to whom in fullest trust and confidence she could bequeath her darling, were she compelled to leave her.

'But you must wait, Harold,' she said. 'My child's nature is one neither to be controlled nor easily satisfied. I can trace her father's tameless soul in her. Poor Pollie! it's a thousand pities that she was not born a boy, as she says herself. How much easier life would have been for her—and for me!' Here Mrs. Devereux sighed.

'All very well, my dear Mrs. Devereux, but in the meantime nature chose to mould her in the form of a beautiful woman, so sweet and lovely in my eyes that I have never seen her equal, and indeed hardly imagined such a creation. She will pass through the unsettled time of girlhood in another year or two, and after that take pity upon her faithful slave and worshipper, who has adored her all his life and who will die in the same faith.'

'That is the worst feature in your case, my poor Harold,' said Mrs. Devereux; 'I am as fond of you as if you were my own son, and she loves you like a brother. You have seen too much of each other. Women's fancies are caught by the unknown, the unfamiliar: we are all alike. I wish I could help you, or bend her to my wish like another girl, for I *know* how happy she would be. But she cannot be guided in the disposition of her affections.'

'And I should not wish it,' said the young man, as his face grew hard. 'No, though I should die of the loss of her.'

The contract time of the Wannonbah mail was indulgent. The driver had no particular reason to reach that somewhat prosaic and monotoned village before the stated hour. When Wanderer slackened speed a mile on the hither side of the Corindah gate, it was with some surprise that Pollie descried a strange four-in-hand converging from another point. Wanderer pricked up his ears, while his rider looked eagerly across the plain with the intense, far-searching gaze of a dweller in the desert, as if she had power to read, even at that distance, each sign and symbol of the equipage.

'Can't be a coach, surely,' she soliloquised. 'One mail is more than enough for all our wants in the letter and passenger way. Cobb and Co. grumble at feeding their teams now, poor things! Who in the world is likely to drive four horses in a season like this? No one but a lunatic, I should think. Such well-bred ones too! I can see the leaders tossing their heads—a grey and a bay. I can't make out the wheelers for the dust. No! Yes! Now I know who it is. Oh, what fun! I beg his pardon. Of course it's Jack Charteris. He said he was going to town. Poor Jack! I wish I was going with him. But that *won't* do. I should like to go and meet him, only then he would make sure I was interested in him. What a misfortune it is to be a girl! Now I must go in and dress for the evening, and receive him properly, which means unnaturally and artificially. Come along, Wanderer!'

When Mr. Jack Charteris swept artistically and accurately through the entrance gate and drew up before the stable range with a fixed expectation that some one might see and admire him, he was disappointed to observe no one but Mr. Gateward and a black boy. To them it was left to perform the *rôle* of spectators, audience, and sympathisers generally.

'Why, Gateward, old man, what's the meaning of this?' said the charioteer, signing to his own black urchin to jump down. 'Are you and Tarpot all the men left alive on Corindah? Sad effects of a dry season and overstocking, eh? No rouse-abouts, no boundary riders, no new chums, no nobody? Family gone away too? I'm not going to ruin you in the forage line either. Brought my own feed—plenty of corn and chaff inside the drag. Don't intend to eat my friends out of house and home this beastly season.'

By this time Mr. Gateward and the black boys had applied themselves with a will to the unharnessing of the team, so that the new-comer, who had uttered the preceding remarks, exclamations, and inquiries in a loud, cheerful, confident manner, threw down his reins and descended from his seat without more ado.

Here he stood with his hands in his pockets, watching the taking out of his horses, a well-bred, well-matched, and well-conditioned team, never intermitting a flow of badinage and small-talk which seemed to proceed from him without effort and forethought.

'Now then, Jerry, you put 'em that one harness along a peg, two feller leader close up, then two feller poler. Tie 'em up long a post, that one yarraman, bimeby get 'um cool, baal gibit water, else that one die. You put 'em feed along a manger all ready. Mine come out bimeby.'

'I'll see after 'em, Mr. Charteris, don't you bother yourself,' said the overseer good-naturedly. 'Tarpot, you take 'em saddle-box belong a mahmee inside barracks. He'll show you, sir,—you know where the bathroom is. There's water there, though we are pretty short.'

'Deuced glad to hear it. The dust's inside my skin like the wool bales last summer. Must be half an inch of it somewhere. I've been living in it all day. Frightful season! I'm just going down to file my schedule—fact—unless my banker takes a good-natured fit. Can't stand it much longer. Ladies well? Mrs. Devereux and Miss Pollie? Not got fever, or cholera, or consumption this God-forsaken summer?'

24

The grave bushman smiled. 'I doubt we shall all have to go up King Street when *you* give in, Mr. Charteris! You can work it somehow or other, whoever goes under. Besides, rain ain't far off; can't be now. The ladies are all right, and a little cheering up won't hurt 'em. Miss Pollie was out for a gallop just before you came up.'

'Then it was her I saw,' said the young man petulantly. 'Knocked smoke out of the team to catch her up, and missed her after all.'

Mr. Jack Charteris, of Monda, was a young squatter who lived about a hundred miles to the west of Corindah, where he had a large and valuable station, a good deal diminished as to profits by the present untoward season. He was of a sanguine, intrepid, rather speculative disposition, having investments in new country as well. People said he had too many irons in the fire, and would probably be ruined unless times changed. But more observant critics asserted that under careless speech and manner Jack Charteris masked a cool head and calculating brain; that he was not more likely to go wrong than his neighbours—in fact, less so, being of uncommon energy and quite inexhaustible resource. With any decent odds he was a safe horse to back to land a big stake.

For the rest he was a good-looking, athletic, cheery young fellow, in general favour and acceptation with ladies, having a great fund of good spirits and an unfailing supply of conversation, that most of his feminine acquaintances found agreeable. He was not easily daunted, and added the qualities of perseverance and a fixed belief in his persuasive powers to the list of his good qualities.

The past masters in the science of conquest aver that the chief secret of fascination lies in the power to amuse the too often vacant and *distraite* feminine mind. Women suffer, it is asserted, more from dulness and ennui than from all other sources, injuries and disabilities put together. Consider, then, at what an enormous advantage he commences the siege who is able to surprise, to interest, to entertain the emotional, laughter-loving garrison, so often in the doldrums, so indifferently able to fill up the lingering hours. It is not the 'rare smile' which lights up the features of the dark and melancholy hero of the Byronic novelists which is so irresistible. Much more dangerous is the jolly, nonsensical, low-comedy person, in whose jokes the superior, the gifted rival can see no wit, indeed but little fun. Thackeray is true to life when he makes Miss Fotheringay unbend to Foker's harmless mirth, rewarding him with a make-believe box on the ear, while Pen, the sombre and dramatic, stands sulkily aloof.

This being an axiomatic truth, Mr. Charteris should have had, to use his own idiom, a considerable 'pull' in commending himself to the good graces of

Miss Devereux, being one of those people to whom women always listened, and never without being more or less amused. But though he would hardly have sighed in vain at the feet of any of the *demoiselles* of the day, rural or metropolitan, he found this particular princess upon whom he had perversely set his heart, unapproachable within a certain clearly defined limit.

Not that she did not like him, respect, admire, even in certain ways to the extent of fighting his battles when absent, praising up his good qualities, delicately advising him for his good, laughing heartily at his good stories and running fire of jests and audacious compliments. That made it so hard to bear. The very fearlessness and perfect candour of her nature forbade him to hope that any softer feeling lay underneath the frankly expressed liking, and a natural dignity which never quitted her restrained him from urging his suit more decisively.

CHAPTER III

When Mr. Charteris had concluded his ablutions, and sauntered into the verandah after a careful toilette, he there encountered Miss Devereux, who, having arrayed herself in a light Indian muslin dress, gracefully reclined upon one of the Cingalese couches. His lonely life of late may have had something to do with it, but his ordinary well-maintained equilibrium nearly failed him before the resistless force of her charms.

Her eyes involuntarily brightened as she partly raised herself from the couch and held out her hand with unaffected welcome. He took in at one rapturous glance her slender yet wondrously moulded form, her delicate hand, her rounded arm seen through the diaphanous fabric, her massed and shining hair, her eloquent face.

'Oh, Lord!' he inwardly ejaculated, as he afterwards confessed. 'I used to wonder at fellows shooting themselves about a girl, and all that, and laugh at the idea. But I don't now. When I saw Pollie Devereux that evening I could have done the maddest thing in the world for the ghost of a chance of winning her. And to win, and wear, and lose her again, as happens to a man here and there. Good heavens' why, it would make a fellow—make—me—run amuck like a Malay, and kill a town full of people before I was half satisfied.'

But Mr. Charteris controlled those too impetuous feelings, and forced himself to remark, as he clasped her cool, soft hand despairingly while she expressed her frank pleasure at seeing him, 'Always delighted to come to Corindah, Miss Devereux, you know that. Didn't I see you near the gate as I drove up? Thought you might have come to meet me.'

'Well, so I would,' the young lady answered, with an air of provoking candour, 'only I had been out to see the coach and find out if they'd brought our package from England—presents that came by last mail,—I was so hot and dusty, and thought it was time to go and dress.'

'And I wanted to see how Wanderer looked, too,' quoth he reproachfully; 'you know I always think he could win the steeplechase at Bourke if you'd let me ride him and wear your colours.'

'I couldn't think of that for two reasons,' replied the girl with decision. 'First of all Wanderer might get hurt. Didn't you see that poor Welcome, at Wannonbah races, broke his leg and had to be shot? I should die, or go into a decline, if anything happened to Wanderer. And then there's another reason.'

'What's that?' inquired Mr. Charteris, with less than his usual intrepidity.

'Why—a—*you* might get hurt, Mr. Charteris, you see, and I can't afford to lose an old friend that way.'

'Oh, is that all?' retorted Master Jack, recovering his audacity; 'well, you could have me shot like Wanderer if I broke my back or anything. 'Pon my soul! it would come to just the same thing if you ordered me out to execution before the race.'

'Now, Mr. Charteris!' said Pollie, in a steady, warning voice, 'you are disobeying orders, you know. I shall hand you over to mother, who has just come to say tea is ready. Mother, he is talking most childish nonsense about shooting himself.'

'But I never talk anything else, do I Mrs. Devereux?' said the young gentleman, running up to the kindly matron with a look of sincere affection. 'Your mother's known me all my life, Miss Devereux, and she won't believe any harm of me. Will you, my dear madam?'

'I never hear of you *doing* any foolish thing, my dear Jack,' said Mrs. Devereux maternally; 'and as long as that is the case I shall not be very angry at anything you can say. We all know you mean no harm. Don't we, Pollie? And now take me into tea, and you may amuse us as much as ever you like. I'm rather low myself on account of the season.'

'No use thinking about it,' quoth Charteris, dashing gallantly into the position assigned to him. 'That's why I'm going to Sydney to have a regular carnival, also to be in time to get the wires to work directly the drought breaks up. I can't make it rain, now can I? And I've a regular tough, steady overseer, a sort of first cousin to your Joe Gateward, with twice as much sense and work in him as I have. I mean to take it easy at the Club till he wires me: "Drought over. Six inches rain." Left the telegram all ready written and pinned up over his desk. He's nothing to do but fill in the number of inches and sign it, and I shall know what to do. That shows faith, doesn't it?'

'But isn't it rather mad to go to Sydney with a four-in-hand and spend money, when you might be ruined, and all of us?' said Pollie.

'You are too prudent but don't look ahead—like most women, my dear young lady,' replied Jack, in the tone of experienced wisdom. 'Nothing like having a logical mind, which, I flatter myself, I possess. I always think the situation out, as thus:—If we are all going to be ruined—the odds are against it, but still it's on the cards—why not have a real first-class time of enjoyment before the grand smash? The trifling expenditure of a good spree won't make any appreciable difference in the universal bankruptcy. You grant me that, don't you?—Yes, thanks, I will take some more wild turkey. Strange that one should have any appetite this weather, isn't it?'

28

'Not if one rides or drives all day and half the night, as you do, Mr. Charteris,' said Pollie. 'Even talking makes you thirsty, doesn't it? But go on with the logic.'

'Did you ever see me scowl, Miss Pollie? Beware of my ferocious mood. Now we're agreed about this, that five hundred pounds, more or less, makes no difference if you're going to be ruined and lose fifty thousand.'

'I suppose not,' reluctantly assented Mrs. Devereux. 'Still it's money wasted.'

'Money wasted!' exclaimed Mr. Charteris. 'I'm surprised at you, Mrs. Devereux. Think of the delights of yachting in the harbour, of the ocean breeze after this vapour from the pit of—of—Avernus. Knew I should find it in time. Then the evening parties, the dinners at the Club, the races, the lawn-tennis, the cricket matches! The English eleven are to be there. Why, I haven't been down for six whole months. Don't you think rational amusement worth all the money you can pay for it? Would you think a couple of years' ramble on the Continent too dearly bought if we were all able to afford to go together?'

The girl's eyes began to glow at this. 'Oh mother!' she said, 'surely we shall be able to go some day. Do you think this horrid drought will stop the possibility of it altogether? If I was sure of that I believe I should drown myself—no, I couldn't do that; but I would burn myself in a bush fire. That's a proper Australian notion of suicide. Water's too scarce and expensive. Think of the consequences if I spoiled a tank. I should like to see Mr. Gateward's face.'

And here the wilful damsel, having at first smiled at the alarmed expression of her mother's countenance, abandoned herself to childish merriment at the ludicrous idea of a drowned maiden in a bad season intensifying the bitterness in the minds of economical pastoralists with the reflection that a flock of sheep would probably be deprived thereby of that high-priced luxury in a dry country—a sufficiency of water.

Mr. Charteris laughed heartily for a few minutes, and then, with sudden solemnity, turned upon the young lady. 'You never will be serious, you know. Why can't you take pattern by me? Let us pursue our argument. Pleasure being worth its price, let us pay it cheerfully. I was reading about the Three Hundred, those Greek fellows you know, dressing their hair before Thermopylæ; it gave me the idea, I think. Mine's too short'—here he rubbed his glossy brown pate, canonically cropped. 'But the principle's the same, Miss Pollie, eh?'

'What principle?' echoed Pollie, 'or want of it, do you mean?'

'The principle of dying game, Miss Devereux,' returned Charteris, with a steady eye and heroic pose. 'Surely you can respect that? It all resolves itself into this. I'm going to put down my ace. If the cards go wrong I have played a dashing game. If the season turns up trumps I'll make the odd trick. You'll see who has the cream of the store sheep-market when the drought breaks!'

'I admire bold play, and you have my best wishes, Mr. Charteris. You've explained everything so clearly. Don't you think if you read history a little more it might lead you to still more brilliant combinations?'

'If you'd only encourage me a little,' answered the young man, with a touch of unusual humility.

'Isn't that Jack Charteris?' said a man's voice in the passage. 'I'll swear I heard him talking about his ace. May I come in, or is there a family council or anything?'

'Come in, Harold, and don't be a goose,' said Mrs. Devereux; 'you are not going to stand on ceremony here at this or any other time.'

'I've had a longish ride,' said the voice, 'nothing to eat, half a sunstroke, I believe, and my journey for my pains. I'm late for tea besides, though I rode hard—takes one so long to dress. If I was any one else I believe I should be cross. I think you'd better all leave me, and I'll join you in the verandah when I've fed and found my temper.'

'Nothing of the sort, mother; you take out Mr. Charteris and give him good advice, while I see after Mr. Atherstone, and recommend him to begin with the wild turkey while I get him some Bukkulla. What's the reason you've not been near us lately, sir?'

The new-comer was a very tall man, though he did not at first sight give you the idea of being much above the middle size, but Mr. Charteris, who was by no means short, looked so when they stood together. Then you saw that he was much above the ordinary stature of mankind. His frame was broad and muscular, and there was an air of latent power about his bearing such as gave the impression of perfect confidence, of physical or mental equality to whatever emergency might befall.

Mr. Charteris lingered, and seemed to question the soundness of the arrangement which divided him from the enchantress and reduced him to the placid enjoyment of Mrs. Devereux's always sensible but not exciting conversation.

'Look here, Jack, I can't have you here while I'm dining, you know,' persisted Mr. Atherstone, with a calm decision. 'You've such an energetic, highly organised nature, you know, that calm people like me can't sustain your electric currents. I perceive by the appearance of that turkey that I'm about to dine in comfort. Pollie has gone to bring in a bottle of Bukkulla. "Put it to yourself carefully," as Mr. Jaggers says, that I have had no lunch. She will be quite as much as I can bear during such a delicate period. So out you go. Order him off, Mrs. Devereux, if you've any pity for me.'

'Well, you are the coolest ruffian, I must say,' quoth Mr. Charteris, as Pollie reappeared bearing a dusty bottle of the cool and fragrant Bukkulla. 'Mrs. Devereux, you spoil him. It's very weak of you. You'll have people talking.'

'We don't mind what people say, do we, Harold?' said the widow, as she watched him carefully draw the cork of the bottle, while Pollie sat near and placed a large hock glass before him. 'Leave them alone for half an hour. I'm sure, poor fellow, he's awfully tired and hungry. I know where he's been; it was on an errand of mine; Mr. Gateward couldn't go. Surely you can put up with my company for a little while.'

'Poor Harold!' grumbled Jack, 'he is to be pitied indeed! Mrs. Devereux, you know I always say there's no one talks so charmingly as you do, and I always say what I mean. Now isn't there something I can do for you in Sydney?'

The symposium thus ostentatiously heralded did not take quite so long as might have been expected, and Pollie, making her appearance in the drawing-room apparently before its termination, went to the piano at Mr. Charteris's instigation, and sang two or three of his favourite songs in a fashion which brought any lingering remnants of his passion once more to the surface. Mr. Atherstone was also good enough to express his approval from the dining-room, the door of which was open, and to request that she would reserve her importation from the metropolis until he came in. This exhortation was followed by his personal apparition, when the latest composition of Stephen Adams was selected by him and duly executed.

Among the natural endowments lavished upon this young creature was such a voice as few women possess, few others adequately develop or worthily employ. Rich, flexible, with unusual compass, depth, and power, it combined strangely mingled tones, which carried with them smiles or tears, hate, defiance, love and despair, the child's glee, the woman's passion; all were enwrapped in this wondrous organ, prompt to appear when the magician touched her spirit with his wand. Harold once said that in her ordinary mood all the glories of vocal power seemed imprisoned in her soul, like the tunes that were frozen in the magic horn.

Men were used to sit with heads bent low, lest the faintest note might escape their highly wrought senses. Grizzled war-worn veterans had wept unrestrainedly as she sang the simple ballads that recalled their youth. Women even were deeply affected, and could not find one word of delicatest depreciation that would sound otherwise than sacrilegious. This was one of her good nights, her amiable, well-behaved nights, Harold said. So the men sat and smoked in the verandah, with Mrs. Devereux near them; all in silence or low, murmuring converse, while the stars burnt brightly in the blue eternity of the summer night—the season itself in its unchanging brightness an emblem of the endless procession of creation—while the girl's melodious voice, now low and soft, now wildly appealing, tender or strong, rose and fell, or swelled and died away—'like an angel's harp,' said Harold to her mother, as she arose and came towards them; 'and it is specially fortunate for us here,' he continued, 'as the season is turning us all into something like the other thing.'

'Hush, Harold, my boy; have faith in God's providence!' replied Mrs. Devereux, placing her hand on his. 'We have been sorely tried at times, but that hope and faith have never failed me.'

'What a lovely, glorious, heavenly night!' said the girl, stepping out on the broad walk which wound amid the odorous orange-trees, still kept in leaf and flower by profuse watering. 'What a shame that one should have to go to bed! I feel too excited to sleep. That is why you fortunate men smoke, I suppose? It calms the excitable nervous system, if you ever suffer in that way.'

'Ask Jack,' said Mr. Atherstone; 'he is more delicately organised. I suppose I like smoking, because I do it a good deal. It is a contemplative, reflective practice, possessing at the same time a sedative effect. It prevents intemperate cerebration. It arrests the wheels of thought, which are otherwise apt to go round and round when there's nothing for them to do—mills with no corn to grind.'

'I never heard so many good reasons before for what many people call a bad habit,' said Pollie. 'However, I must say, considering the hard work you poor fellows have to do at times, I think a man enjoying his pipe after his day's work a dignified and ennobling spectacle.'

'Quite my idea, Miss Pollie,' said Jack. 'I really thought my brain was giving way once in a dry season. If I hadn't smoked, should have had to fall back upon drinking. Dreadful to think of, isn't it? A mixture of Latakia and Virginia I got from a fellow down from India on leave saved my life.'

'I think we are all sufficiently soothed and edified now to go to bed,' said Mrs. Devereux, with mild, suggestive authority. 'Dear me! nearly twelve o'clock too. The days are so long now that it is ever so late before dinner is finished and the evening fairly begun.'

32

The parcel from England to which reference had been made on the occasion of Pollie's excursion to Mogil Mogil clump had arrived safely, and its contents been duly admired, when a letter received by the next mail-steamer contained such exceptional tidings that all other incidents became tame and uninteresting.

This English letter proved to be from Captain Devereux's elder brother, with whom, since the former's death, Mrs. Devereux had kept up a formal but regular correspondence. The members of her husband's family had proved sympathetic in her hour of sorrow. They had possibly been touched by the passionate grief of a relative whose letters after a while commenced to exhibit so much sound sense and proper feeling. From that time the elders of the house of Devereux never omitted befitting attention and friendly recognition of the far-off, unknown kinswoman.

And now, it seems, they had despatched Mr. Bertram Devereux, late lieutenant in Her Majesty's 6th Dragoon Guards, who, from force of circumstances, reckless extravagance and imprudence no doubt, but from no improper conduct, had been compelled to quit that crack corps and the brilliant society he adorned. He had a small capital, however, several thousand pounds fortunately, the bequest of an aunt. Having decided upon a colonial career, he was anxious to gain the requisite experience on the estate of his cousin, Mrs. Brian Devereux. If she had no objection, would she lay them all under a deep obligation by receiving the young man into her family, and by acting a mother's part to one who was forced to quit home and native land, perhaps for ever?'

This last enclosure was from Lady Anne Devereux, a lady in her own right, who, much to the distaste of her friends and family, had been fascinated by the handsome Colonel Dominick Daly Devereux, one of the military celebrities of the day. In the main the tone of the letter was proud and cold; but there were a few expressions which so plainly showed the mother's bruised heart, that Mrs. Devereux could not resist the appeal.

'I fear he will be a troublesome inmate in one sense or another,' she reflected. 'He is hardly young enough to take kindly to station life. Then again, how will my darling girl be affected by his companionship? But I can enter into a mother's feelings. I cannot refuse hospitality to my dear husband's nephew. We must make the best of it. He will not be worse, I suppose, than other newly arrived young men. They are an awful bother during the first year. After that they become like other people. I hope Mr. Gateward will take to him.'

And now the stated time had been over-passed. The *Indus* (P. and O. Service) had arrived; a telegram had been received; and Mr. Bertram Devereux was hourly expected by the mail-coach. This fateful vehicle did actually arrive rather late on the evening specified, it is true, but without having, according to Pollie's prophecies and reiterated assertions, either broken down, upset, or lost its way owing to the new driver taking a back track which led into the wilderness and ended at a lately finished tank, far from the habitations of civilised man.

As the coach swung round the corner of the stock-yard and drew up underneath a wide-branched white acacia which shaded a large proportion of an inner enclosure, the driver received a *douceur* which confirmed him in the opinion which he had previously entertained of his passenger being 'a perfect gentleman.' He therefore busied himself actively in unloading his portmanteau and other effects, deposited the station mail-bag, and without further loss of time took the well-trodden road to the township. As the eyes of his late fare rested mechanically upon the fast-departing coach, he saw little but a cloud of dust outlining every turn of the road, amid which gleamed the five great lamps, which finally diminished apparently into star-fragments, as they traversed the unending plain which stretched northward and northward ever.

A young man, whose Crimean shirt and absence of necktie denoted to the traveller the presumed abandon of bush life, advanced from the door of a species of shop for general merchandise, as it seemed to the stranger, and dragging in the mail-bag, saluted him courteously. 'Mr. Devereux, I think? Please to come in.'

Meekly following his interlocutor through the 'shop,' as he termed it, he found himself in a smaller and more comfortable room. Looking around at the somewhat 'cabin'd, cribb'd, and confin'd' section, he answered, 'My name is Devereux. I have come to remain. May I ask which of these rooms is to be allotted to me?'

The storekeeper smiled. 'You didn't think this was the house, sir? This is the overseer's place, the barracks, as we call it in the bush. If you come after me I'll show you the way. Your luggage will be brought to you if you will leave it here.'

The new-comer had not, in truth, troubled himself to consider what Australian dwellings might resemble. He expected nothing. He had made up his mind to the worst. Therefore he would not have been in the least surprised if his aunt or cousin had issued from one of the small apartments which opened out from the larger room; had directed him to occupy another; had then and there placed a kettle on the smouldering wood fire for the purpose of providing him with refreshment after his journey.

He therefore mechanically followed his guide through a passage and along a verandah until they reached a white gate in a garden paling, when the young man in the light raiment quitted him with this farewell precept—

'The front entrance is between those two large rose-bushes, and the first room to the right of the hall. Mrs. Devereux or Miss Pollie sure to be there.'

Proceeding along the path as he had been directed, Bertram Devereux commenced to experience a slight degree of surprise, even curiosity. He was evidently in an æsthetic region, short as had been the distance from the sternest commonplace. The borders had been carefully kept. Flowers were blooming profusely. Oranges and limes shed a subtle and powerful odour around. The stars gleamed on a sheet of water which had evidently helped to create this oasis in the desert. The whispering leaves of the banana brought back memories of tropic glories of foliage. Turning between two vast cloth-of-gold standards, the blooms of which met and clustered about his head, he ascended a flight of steps and found himself in a broad verandah furnished with cane lounges and hammocks.

The hanging lamp, which illumined a wide and lofty hall, showed ferns of various size and foliage, the delicate colouring of which struck gratefully upon his aching and dust-enfeebled eyes. A book, a few gathered flowers, lay upon a small table with some half-executed ornamental needlework. All told of recent feminine presence and occupation.

As he lingered in observation of these novelties, a lady passed into the hall from a side-door and advanced with a look of kindly welcome.

'You are Bertram Devereux, I know, and oh! though your hair and eyes are dark'—here she looked wistfully in his face—'I can see the family likeness to my darling husband. You are the only one of his relations I have seen. You may think how welcome you are at Corindah. But it is a lonely life. I am afraid you will miss the society you have been accustomed to. My husband could never have endured it but that he hoped to make a fortune.'

'And so do I, Aunt Mary,' said the young man, with a quiet smile. 'Had I not expected great things I should never have come so far from civilisation. But I should not talk so,' he added, looking round. 'You seem to have everything one has been used to, conservatories and all.'

'We have always tried to live in reasonable comfort,' replied Mrs. Devereux. 'As to the fortune, it is sometimes a long time in coming. And a dry year like this delays it still more. Now, having told you how glad we are to see you, you will be anxious to be shown your bedroom. In half an hour the bell will ring for tea. We do not dine late, but I can promise you something substantial after your journey.'

After a bath and a leisurely change of toilette in the very well appointed bedroom where he was installed—the flowers upon the dressing and writing tables betokening the expected guest—the pilgrim commenced to take a more tolerant view of Australian prospects than up to this period he had deemed possible.

'Quiet, yet dignified and refined woman, my new aunt,' he soliloquised. 'Very far from the bustling farmer's wife I had expected. Handsome in her youth—very—must have been. My erratic cousin was by no means such a fool as we all thought him. And her fair daughter, too—how about her? A beauty and an heiress, they all say. I never bargained for that. Seems as if there were women wherever one goes—wherever I go, at least. Just my luck.'

Mr. Devereux had scarcely enunciated this disheartening truism, with a mildly resigned, not to say desponding expression of countenance, when the bell of which he had been warned rang out a peal. Placing a rosebud of Gloire de Dijon in his button-hole, he sought the drawing-room, of which he found himself the sole occupant.

He had observed that it was handsomely furnished, in a style not noticeably different from the fashion of the day, being not wholly devoid of china, having a few rare plaques and Moorish brass-ware—there was even a dado, also a magnificent grand piano by Erard—when two young people came through one of the French windows which 'gave' into the verandah.

'I shall never agree with you, Harold,' the girl was saying to her companion; 'not even if we lived here for the next twenty years—and I shall drown or otherwise make away with myself in that case.'

'There are worse places than Corindah,' replied a young man who followed her in. 'You may live to be convinced of the fact.'

'I should hate any place,' retorted the girl, in playful defiance, 'if I had to live there all my life. I quite envy my cousin Mr. Devereux, who has only just come. Everything will be so nice and new to him. Cousin Bertram,' she said, advancing and holding out her hand, 'I am charmed to welcome you. Mother and I have been talking of no one else for the last week. Let me introduce Mr. Harold Atherstone, a near neighbour and a great friend of ours. He will be able to give you advice and information beyond all price.'

The two men bowed gravely, as is the manner of freshly acquainted Britons, and looked steadily, if not searchingly, into each other's eyes. The new-comer spoke first.

'I can't tell you how pleased I am with everything—and everybody,' he said, after a slight pause; 'so different from what I had expected. I feel as if I had found a home and relations instead of leaving them for ever. Most happy to meet Mr. Atherstone, and hope to profit by his experience and other people's.'

For the few seconds that passed while the new friend and the old one confronted one another the young lady regarded them keenly. Nor was her mind idle. 'As far as appearance goes,' she thought, 'Harold has certainly the best of it. Tall, well-proportioned, with nice brown hair and beard, and those honest grey eyes—what most girls would call a splendid fellow, and so he is. Why am I not fonder of him? Bertram is certainly distinguished looking, but he is only middle-sized and almost plain—dark hair and eyes, rather good these last. I feel disappointed; I don't know why. He smiles nicely—that is, he *could* if he took the trouble. We must wait, I suppose, till his character develops. I hate waiting. I see mother coming. We had better go in to tea.'

This last observation was the only one audible. The other results of lightning-like apprehension had only been flashed by electric agencies from eye and heart to brain—there registered, doubtless, for future verification or erasure, as circumstances might determine. Mrs. Devereux had entered. Pollie offered her arm to her cousin, whom she piloted to the dining-room, leaving Mr. Atherstone to follow with her mother.

If the young *émigré* had been previously astonished at the tone of the household arrangements, he was even more surprised as he surveyed the well-lighted room and marked with much inward satisfaction the well-served repast, the complete and elegant table appointments. The tea equipage at the head of the table, over which Mrs. Devereux presided, determined the character of the repast; but the general effect was that of a sufficiently good dinner, with adjuncts of light wine and the pale ale of Britain, which neither of the young men declined. Both ladies were becomingly dressed in evening costume—Mrs. Devereux plainly and unobtrusively, while her daughter had donned for the occasion a sea-green mermaiden triumph of millinery, which subtly suited the delicate tints of her complexion, as also the silken masses of her abundant hair.

In the trial of first introductions, unless the key-note be swiftly struck and more than one of the talkers be enthusiastic, the conversation is apt to languish, being chiefly tentative and fragmentary. Now Pollie was eagerly enthusiastic, but her burning impatience on a score of subjects awoke no responsive note in the incurious, undemonstrative kinsman. He was apparently ready to receive information about the customs of a country and people to him so novel, but did not press for it.

He studiously avoided committing himself to opinions, and made but few assertions. On the other hand, Harold Atherstone declined to pose as a didactic or locally well-informed personage, contenting himself with remarking that those intending pastoralists who possessed common sense acquired information for themselves; to the other division advice was useless and experience vain. This cynical summing up of the Great Australian Question merely caused the stranger to raise his eyebrows, and Pollie to pout and declare that Mr. Atherstone was very disobliging and quite unlike himself that evening.

Upon this it appeared to Mrs. Devereux to interpose an apologetic observation concerning the state of the country, including the roads, live-stock, and pasturage; to which their guest made answer that he had always believed Australia to be a dry and parched region, and had supposed this to be a normal state of matters.

'Oh! we're not quite so bad always as you see us now,' exclaimed Pollie, suppressing a laugh. 'Are we, Harold? You would hardly believe that these dusty plains are covered with grass as high as a horse's head in a good season, would you now?'

Mr. Devereux did *not* believe it. But he inclined his head politely and said that it must present a very pleasing appearance.

'Yes, indeed,' continued the girl. 'In the old days the shepherds were provided with horses, because the grass was so tall that the sheep used to get lost. Men on foot could not see them in it.'

The listener began to feel convinced that the facts related were approaching the border of strange travel and adventure so circumstantially described by one Lemuel Gulliver, but he manfully withheld utterance of the heresy, merely remarking that they would think that very strange in England.

'I'm afraid you're cautious,' quoth his fair teacher, trying to frown. 'If there's anything I despise, it's caution. It's your duty as a newly arrived person to be wildly astonished at anything, to make quantities of mistakes, and so gradually to learn the noble and aristocratic profession of a squatter. If you're going to be unnaturally rational, I shall have no pleasure in teaching you.'

'If *you* will undertake the task,' replied the neophyte, with a sudden gleam in his dark eyes which for an instant lighted up the somewhat sombre countenance, 'I will promise to commit all the errors you may think necessary.'

'As to that, we'll see,' answered the damsel, with a fine affectation of carelessness. 'I make no promises. We shall have plenty of time—Oh, dear! what quantities of it we do waste here—to find out all one another's bad qualities. Shall we not, Harold?'

'I have never made any discoveries of the sort, Miss Devereux,' said the young man; 'I can't answer, of course, for the result of your explorations.'

'I couldn't find anything bad in you,' said the girl eagerly, 'if I tried for a century. That's the worst of it. You always put me in the wrong. Doesn't he, mother? There's no satisfaction in quarrelling with him.'

'Why should you quarrel if it comes to that?' queried the matron, with a wistful glance at her child. 'You only differ in opinion occasionally, I observe.'

'Why, because quarrelling is one of the necessities—I should almost say luxuries—of existence,' retorted the young lady. 'What would life be without it? Think of the pleasure of making it up. I should die if I didn't quarrel with somebody now and then.'

'Or talk nonsense occasionally, as your cousin has doubtless by this time observed,' answered her mother. 'I think we may adjourn to the drawing-room.'

The drawing-room in this case meant the verandah, in which luxurious retreat the little party soon ensconced themselves.

'Really,' remarked Devereux, as he lit a cigar and abandoned himself to the inner depths of a Cingalese chair, 'if there was a little motion, I could fancy we were in the Red Sea. Same sky, same stars, same mild temperature, and tobacco. This is very different from the stern realities of colonial life I had pictured to myself.'

'We don't give ourselves out as industrial martyrs,' remarked Atherstone placidly, 'but you will probably find out that bush life is not all beer and skittles.'

'Hope not,' replied Devereux. 'That would be too good to last, obviously. Still I can gather that you have extenuating circumstances. I certainly never expected to spend my first evening like this.'

Atherstone made no answer, but apparently permitted his pipe reverie to prevail. The other man reclined as if somewhat fatigued, and smoked his cigar, listening indolently to the running conversational comment which his cousin kept up, sometimes with him, sometimes with Atherstone, whose answers were chiefly monosyllabic. The girl's fresh voice falling pleasantly upon his ear, with the lulling effect of rhythmic melody or murmuring stream, Mr. Bertram Devereux was led to the conclusion, by his novel and interesting experience, that an evening might be spent pleasantly, even luxuriously, at this incredible 'distance from town,' as he himself would have expressed it.

With this conviction, however, and the termination of his cigar came a distinctly soporific proclivity, so that, pleading fatigue and declining further refreshment, the new-comer was fain to betake himself to bed, in which blessed refuge from care and pain, labour and sorrow, he shortly ceased to revolve the very comprehensive subject of colonial experience.

CHAPTER IV

On the morning after his arrival the visitor, making his appearance at an early hour, had a short conversation with Mr. Gateward, whom he found at the horse-yard sending out his men for the day. 'Of course I know nothing of this sort of thing,' he said; 'but I have come here to learn, with a view to investing a few thousands I have in a property, or station, as I think you call it. Now understand clearly that I shall be glad to help in the work of the place, in any way that I am fitted for. I can ride and drive decently, shoot, walk, keep accounts; in a general way do most things that other people can. Of course I can't pick up the whole drill at once, but I don't want you to spare me. I came to Australia to work, and the sooner I learn the better.'

'All right, sir,' replied the bronzed veteran, 'I'll see what I can do. If you ride about with me every day, and keep your eyes open, you'll pick up as much in six months as most of the people know that own stations. It's a bad year now, and we're all in the doldrums, as the sailors say. But it's not going to be that way always. The wind'll change or the rain'll come, and then we'll be able to show you what Corindah looks like in a good season.'

'Then we understand each other. I'll take my orders from you, but, of course, from no one else—('Not likely,' interjected Mr. Gateward, looking at the steady eye and short, proud upper lip of the speaker)—'and early or late, wet or dry (if it ever *is* wet here), hot or cold, you'll find me ready and willing. Give me a couple of good hacks, and I'll soon have an idea of how you carry on the war.'

'I'm dashed sure you will, sir, and I shall be proud to help a gentleman like you to a knowledge of things, that's willing to learn, and not too proud to take a hint.'

'Quite so. I suppose you remember my cousin Brian? I was very young when he left home, but I always heard that he was a hard man to beat at anything he chose to go in for.'

'He was as fine a man as ever wore shoe-leather,' said the overseer. 'Everybody respected him in these parts, and he was that jolly and kind in his ways, nobody could help liking him. If he hadn't been cut off in his prime by that infernal Doctor—the cattle-duffing, horse-stealing hound—he'd have been one of the richest men in the district this very minute.'

'He was shot by a highway robber?' inquired Devereux; 'what you call a bushranger in Australia, don't you?'

'Well, there are bushrangers and bushrangers,' said the overseer. 'This chap, the Doctor, hadn't regularly took to the bush, as one might say, though he was worse than many as did. He belonged to a mob of cattle-stealers that used to duff cattle in the back country, and pass them over to Queensland. Well, Mr. Tracknell, one of the squatters in the back blocks, began to run 'em pretty close, and put the police on 'em. They heard he was to be in the coach from Orange on a certain day, and made it right to stick it up and give him a lesson.'

'What's sticking up?'

'Well, sir, by what one hears and reads, it is what used to be called "stopping" on the Queen's highway in England.'

'Then they had no grudge against Brian Devereux?'

'Not a bit in the world. He was known far and wide as a free-handed gentleman. Any one was welcome to stop at Corindah in his time, and no poor man ever went away hungry. The man the Doctor and Bill Bond wanted wasn't in the coach as it happened. He'd got wind of it and cleared. But they heard there was a gentleman with a big beard going down the country, and made sure it was him. When they came up and saw their mistake, they'd have rode off again, only the Captain was that hot-tempered and angry at their stopping him, that he fired on them, and nearly collared the lot. They returned it, and rode off as well as they could, and never knew till days after that they had hit him. Them as told me said the Doctor was devilish sorry for it, and that he was the last man in the district they'd have hurt.'

'What became of the Doctor, as you call him?'

'Well, sir, he's in the back country somewhere in Queensland yet, I believe. He served a sentence for horse-stealing of seven years; but he's wanted again, and there's a warrant out for him. He's a desperate man now, and I wouldn't be sure he won't do something that'll be talked about yet before his end comes.'

'It's to be hoped there'll be a rope round his neck on that day,' said Bertram; 'scoundrels of that kind should be trapped or poisoned like vermin.'

'Well, sir, the Doctor's no chop, but there's worse than Bill Bond, if you'll believe me. The only thing is, now he's hunted from pillar to post so, and he ain't got half a chance to repent if he wanted ever so much, I'm afraid he'll do something out of the way bad yet.'

The autumnal season, with calm sun-gilded days, cool starlight, unclouded nights, and mornings fresh and exhilarating, as if newly ordered from Paradise, came gradually to an end. Lovely, passing fair, as weather in the abstract; but dry, dry, always dry, and as such lamentable and injurious. Then winter made believe to arrive with the first week in June. But how could it be winter, Bertram thought, when the skies were still cloudless and untroubled, the mid-day warm, the plains dusty, the air soft, the river low; when the flowers in the garden bloomed and budded as usual; when no leaf fell from the forest; when, save the great acacias in the backyard and the white cedars in the garden, all the trees at Corindah were green and full-foliaged? The chief difference was that the nights were longer, cooler. There were sharp frosts from time to time; and when Bertram arose early in the morning, according to his wont, all things were covered with an icy mantle. On one occasion, when he met Mr. Gateward coming in from a long night ride, his abundant beard was frozen stiff as a stalactite.

The sheep died faster than ever, at which Bertram wondered much, but did not ask questions. 'Everything comes to him who waits,' was one of his favourite proverbs.

'If it had been always thus,' he told himself, 'so many evidences of capital and prosperity would not be here. A change will come sometime, but I cannot hasten it by ignorant questions. I shall learn all about this extraordinary country in the course of time.'

His theory was sound. But Mrs. Devereux was neither so self-contained nor philosophical. She complained and bemoaned herself from time to time, as is the way of women. At the evening meal, when after the day's duties the two young people and herself met with an affectation of social enjoyment, she made many things plain to the inquiring mind of Bertram Devereux, silent and incurious as he seemed to be.

'It had not always been thus. In the old, happy days droughts had certainly occurred, but with intervals of years between. Now the seasons seemed to have changed. The year before last was a drought, and now—this was the most sore and terrible grass famine she had ever remembered. Their losses would be frightful, disastrous, ruinous.'

'Was it on the cards that she would be actually ruined—lose all her property, that is—if the season remained unchanged?'

'Well, not absolutely. She could not truthfully say that. Even if all the sheep on Corindah died, the whole fifty thousand, the land and fences would remain. But twenty or thirty thousand pounds would be an immense sum to make up. The very thought made her shudder. To think of the years it had taken to make and save it! No doubt she could get more sheep. Her credit, she was thankful to say, was good enough for that.'

'I believe it's all Mr. Gateward's fault, said Pollie impetuously. 'Why did he persuade you not to buy a station in the mountains last year, where there's beautiful green grass and running water in the driest summer. That's what is needed for the poor sheep now. And all for a thousand pounds.'

'A thousand pounds is a great deal of money,' said Mrs. Devereux. 'He thought he could get some country cheaper, and in the meantime it was snapped up. I have been sorry for it ever since. But he meant well, as he always does.'

'I know that. He's as good an old creature as ever lived, and devoted to you and me, mother. I wouldn't say a word against him for the world. But he's too slow and cautious in matters like this, which need decision. Think of all the poor weak sheep, with their imploring eyes, that would have been kept alive if we had sent twenty or thirty thousand up to those lovely mountains.'

'I suppose it's too late now,' said Bertram. 'Of course I know nothing as yet, but could not some of them—ten thousand or so—be taken away now?'

'That's where the misery is,' said Pollie. 'The snow has fallen on the mountains. Indeed, nearly all the sheep have come away. Those thirty thousand of Mr. Haller's that passed here last week, and gave you so much trouble, had just come from there. And how nice and strong they were, do you remember? Our poor things are so weak that they couldn't travel if we had ever so much green grass to send them to.'

'It's Napoleon's Russian campaign over again—only, that our country's too dry to hold us, and his was too cold. And is there no return from Elba?'

'When the rain comes, not before. It may come soon, in a few months, this year, next year, not at all. So we're in a pleasing state of uncertainty, don't you think?'

'And you are not all sitting in sackcloth and ashes, or fasting, or making vows to the saints, and what not! This is a wonderful country, and you are wonderful people, I must say, to take matters so calmly.'

'We know our country and the general course of the seasons,' said Mrs. Devereux. 'In the long-run they prove favourable, though the exceptional years are hard. And we strive to have faith in God's providence, believing that whoso trusts in Him will not be left desolate.'

Letter from Miss M. A. Devereux to Miss Clara Thornton, Fairoaks, Edgecliffe, Sydney:—

MY DARLING CLARA—I hope you think of me daily, nightly, at breakfast and lunch time; also at midnight, when you can look out of your bedroom window, and see that lovely South Head beacon-light and the star-showers gleaming on the wavelets of the bay; when you can inhale the strong sweet ocean breath, and dream of far-away tropic isles and palm groves, coral reefs, pirates too, and all the delightful denizens of the world of romance. How you ought to pity me, shut up in poor, dry, dusty Corindah!—the weather going from bad to worse; Mother and Mr. Gateward looking more woebegone every day; and the poor sheep dying at such a rate that even as we sit in the house odours are wafted towards us not exactly of Araby the Blest. Bertie calls it '*bouquet de merino.*'

Who is Bertie? Did I not tell you before? He is the English cousin that has come to live with us and learn how to make a fortune by keeping sheep in Australia. 'What is he like?' of course you ask. Well, he is *not* a great many things. So he is not a hero of romance, ready made for the consolation of your poor friend in this famine year. He is not handsome, nor tall, nor clever—that is, brilliantly so. Not a particular admirer of his poor Australian cousin either. He is very cool and undemonstrative; lets you find out his talents and strong points by degrees, accidentally, as it were. If I were to describe him more accurately than in any other way that occurs to me, I should say he is different from everybody else I have ever seen in this colony—extremely well able to take care of himself under all circumstances, and quite careless as to the effect he produces.

He is very well educated—cultured, I might say; reads and speaks French and German. So, as we have absolutely nothing to do in the evenings, he reads with me, and I get on a great deal faster than any of us did at Miss Watchtower's. You know I have always had a passion for what is called 'seeing the world'; it seems to be born in me, and I can recollect when I was quite a little thing being far more interested in books of travel than any other reading. I really believe that if anything led to the station being sold, and we have any money left after these frightful droughts, that I should persuade mother to take me 'home,' as we Australians always say, and then have a good, satisfactory, leisurely prowl over Europe. Now, do you see what I am coming to? What is the use of seeing everything in dumb show? I intend to work hard, very hard, at languages now I have the chance. Then I shall be able to enjoy life and instruct my mind fully when I do go abroad. Abroad! Rome, Paris, Florence! The idea is too ecstatic altogether. I shall die if it is not realised. I feel as if I should die of joy if it is.

I am writing at my little table in my bedroom. As I look out the moonlight makes everything as clear as day. There is a slight breeze, and I can actually see the dust as it rises on the plain, midwinter though it is supposed to be. I couldn't live here all my life, now could I? Not for all the cattle and sheep in Australia! I don't feel inclined to go to bed. But I suppose I must say good-night to my dearest Clara, and remain your too lonely friend,

POLLIE.

After the first month or two of the excitement caused by the arrival of a 'new chum' at Corindah on the experience ticket, as the vernacular of the West Logan had it, much of the mingled curiosity, doubt, or disapproval with which the emigrant gentleman is usually regarded in a distant provincial circle died away. Of this last attribute of the neophyte Mr. Devereux had incurred but little. Studiously careful of speech, habitually courteous in bearing, and wholly indifferent to general opinion, but few men of those with whom he was brought into contact could find anything upon which to found depreciatory opinion. The utmost that professional carpers and cynics could aver amounted merely to an inability to 'make him out,' as they phrased it, coupled with a lurking suspicion that he 'thought himself a deuced deal too good for the district of West Logan and the people that belonged to it.'

'Confound him!' said Bob Barker, who posed as a leading society man and *arbiter elegantiarum*, 'what right has he to come here and look down on the lot of us as if we were small farmers or country bumpkins? Suppose he *was* in the Guards, there's nothing so wonderful about that. I know his mother was a lady in her own right, but a gentleman is only a gentleman, and other people have relatives in the aristocracy as well as him.'

Here Bob twisted his moustache and looked proudly around the company— squatters, magistrates, and others, a select party of whom, this being Court-day at Wannonbah, had assembled in the parlour of the principal hotel.

'Are you quite sure that he does look down, as you call it, upon all of us fellows, Barker, or did you only think it was ten to one he would?' said one of the assembled magistrates, a native-born Australian, with a slow, monotonous intonation which did injustice to a shrewd intellect and keen sense of humour. 'You know we *are* rather rusty, some of us. We've been so long away from England.' Here the speaker bestowed a wink of preternatural subtlety upon a good-humoured looking, middle-aged man who occupied the chair at the head of the table.

'Rusty be hanged!' said Mr. Barker. 'I could go home and take my position in society to-morrow as if I had never left. I don't want any young military puppy to teach *me* manners.'

'But what—did—he—do, Barker?' inquired the other squatter; 'or—what—did—he—say—that—put—your—monkey—up?'

'Well, of course he didn't do anything, and as for saying, he was infernally polite; but somehow I knew by the quiet, simple way he spoke what he was thinking of. And then, when we were playing whist, Atherstone and I with Miss Devereux and the old lady, he looked on until I asked if he was approved of our play. He smiled faintly, and then begged to know whether "out here" we were always in the habit of leading from our longest suits? I could have kicked him on the spot.'

'But—perhaps—he—only—wanted—to—know,' pursued his tormentor, who now appeared honestly desirous of extracting information. 'You're—so—very—smart—Barker, yourself—you—know.'

'Oh, I dropped down to him,' said Barker. 'They've got some confounded new-fangled way of calling for trumps in these London clubs, and of course, like all English people, he thinks we never hear anything or read anything, and have never seen any society men for a century but himself. Why, wasn't General Burstall here the other day on leave from India? Saw my brother at Simla just the week he left. However, wait till this season's over. That'll take some of the starch out of him.'

'It'll—take—the—starch—out—of—some—of—us—too,' replied the first speaker, 'if—it—doesn't—break—up—soon. I've—lost—six—thousand—pounds—worth—of—cattle—already. Everybody—says—your—frontage—looks—frightful—Bar—ker—eh?'

The intense gravity and slow solemnity with which this sudden assault was performed upon Mr. Barker, impugning the character of his run, and by implication his probable solvency, appeared so overpoweringly ludicrous to the company, that a diversion was effected in favour of Mr. Barker's pasturage, who therefore permitted the personal questions to lapse.

Letter from Bertram Devereux to Captain Goodwood, 6th Dragoon Guards:—

My dear Charlie—Partly on account of a weak promise to let you and one or two more of the old set into the secrets of my other-world life when I said good-bye after that fatal Derby that proved such a smasher, partly because one has such enormous quantities of spare time in the desert here, I am going to produce a respectable despatch—may even go the length of becoming a regular correspondent—while quartered here.

My jottings down, apart from any personal interest which may yet survive the writer's departure, ought to possess a certain value as tidings from a far country—descriptions of a mode of life and state of society of which no one I ever met in England had the faintest idea. It is odd, too, for how many youngsters from good families that we know have emigrated within the last ten years! And with one or two exceptions there was no gleaning any information from their friends. Either the fellows didn't write or had done indifferently, and so the less said the better, or else the friends hardly could tell whether they lived in Victoria, Western Australia, New South Wales, or Tasmania, which is much as if the whereabouts of a continental traveller should be described as indifferently as in Belgium, Berlin, Switzerland, or Sicily. There is a want of exactitude about our countrymen, I must say, in all matters that do not concern their own immediate interests, most painful to persons gifted with a love of method—like you and me, for instance. No wonder we English are always caught unprepared when we go to war, and get laughed at all over Europe—till we begin to fight, that is. The reaction sets in then.

However, *revenons à nos moutons*—a strictly appropriate tag, inasmuch as this lodge in the wilderness is surrounded by enormous estates, leasehold, not freehold, by the way, all devoted to the production of the merino variety of the ovine family. Millions of them are bred in these great solitudes. In favourable years I gather that one is enabled to export about one-half to a fourth of their value, in the shape of wool. This brings a good price, is as negotiable as gold, and the fortunes of the returned colonists that we used to see in London society are thus compiled. Of course there are details, the which I am setting my mind to master. But they would hardly interest you. One trifling fact I may mention, lest you may imagine the progress of fortune-constructing too ridiculously easy. It is, that there has been next to no rain for more than a year, strange, almost incredible, as it may seem to you of the rainy isles. In consequence, the country looks like a desert, and tens of thousands of sheep are dying here, and for hundreds of miles in every direction. Occurrences of this kind, you will understand, delay indefinitely and perhaps wholly frustrate one's too obvious purpose of gathering a competency and hurrying out of the strange country as fast as may be.

'All this is very well,' I hear you say; 'but what about the social system? Why doesn't he tell me about *her*?—for of course there is a woman somewhere within the orbit of his existence. Wonder what they're like out there. Must be some, I suppose.'

With your usual acuteness, which I have rarely known at fault, unless confronted by a plain unvarnished robbery like the doing to death of the favourite (and very nearly the backers) in our fatal year, you have hit the gold.

Well, somehow or other, there *is* a she. How strange it seems that one's life, whether

> 'Pone me pigris ubi nulla campis
> Arbor æstiva recreatur aura,' etc.,

or in the midst of cities, or even in the comparatively assured and fortified privacy of a messroom, should never be wholly free from the invasion of womankind. A book, a photograph, a souvenir of the slightest kind, is sufficient to arouse the tempestuous motives of those who are doomed to be 'the prey of the gods' in this peculiar fashion. How much more so the perfect human form, 'ripe and real,' when it comes before your eyes in all the unconscious temptation of virgin youth and beauty scarce unfolded morning, noon, and night. Add to this that I'm at present *habitans in sicco*, and you will conclude, with the swift logical subtlety so proverbially yours, that as a latter-day hermit I may compare favourably with St. Anthony.

Heaven knows I did not rush into danger. Languid and prostrated as I was after the overthrow of all my worldly hopes; worn and despairing when the one devouring, passionate love of my life had disappeared, and it was like the last scene of a tragedy, when nothing is left for the spectators but to wrap their cloaks around them and go home—I deemed that I was coming to a land where there were no women, except black ones or those required for culinary purposes.

How little we know of these new lands and their inhabitants, all English as they are, as if in the Midland Counties, yet of manner strangely fresh! All is high development and new material. How I am shut up with a magnificent young creature, with a face like Egeria, and a figure like the huntress maid, burning with enthusiasm, talented, cultured, full of all noble feminine attributes; dangerous with the fascinations of fresh, innocent womanhood, yet ignorant of the ways of the world, and childlike in her unsuspicious confidence!

How I wish I was young again! I do really, Charlie. Could I but blot out the years that have intervened—not so many—but what Dead-Sea fruits have I not tasted during their stormy course? What a burnt-out volcano is this heart of mine! Could I but recall the past and be like one of our schoolboy heroes!

> 'The happy page who was the lord
> Of one soft heart and his own sword.'

What empires and kingdoms would I give—supposing them to be mine —to revert to that position, and so prove myself worthy of the fresh heart, the petals of which are about to open before my graduated advance, like a rose in June! That I shall be the favoured suitor, despite of the opposition of a good-looking, stalwart, provincial rival, my experience assures me. With women *l'inconnu* is always the interesting, the romantic, the irresistible. In despite of myself, I can see clearly my future position of *jeune premier* in this opera of the wilderness. It might be worse, you will say. That I grant. But you know that Helen of Troy would never control this restless, wayward heart of mine in perpetuity.

For the rest, the life is bearable enough, free, untrammelled, novel, with a tinge of adventure. My days are spent in the saddle. There's just a hint of shooting, no hunting, no fishing. We dress for dinner, and live much as at a shooting-lodge in the Highlands, with stock-riders for gillies. So we are not altogether barbarous, as you others imagine. This letter is far too long, and imprudently confiding, so I hasten to subscribe myself yours, as of old,

BERTRAM DEVEREUX.

So much for the impression Pollie was capable of producing on a worn, world-weary heart.

It was a strange fate which had thus imprisoned this beautiful creature, so richly endowed with all the attributes which combine to form the restless, tameless, unsatisfied man, amid surroundings so uninteresting and changeless. Eager for adventure, even for danger, she was curious with a child's hungering, insatiable appetite for the knowledge of wondrous lands, cities, peoples; hating the daily monotone to which the woman's household duties are necessarily attuned. Capable of the strongest, the most passionate attachments, yet all-ignorant as yet of the subtle, sweet, o'ermastering tone of the world-conquering harmony of love. In the position to which she appeared immovably attached by circumstance, she seemed like a strayed bright-plumaged bird, a foreign captive, taken in infancy and reared in an alien land.

A chamois in a sheepfold, a leopardess in a drawing-room, a red deer in a trim and close-paled enclosure, could not have been more hopelessly at war with surroundings, more incongruously provided with food and shelter. Day after day a growing discontent, a hopeless despair of life, seemed to weigh her down, to take the savour from existence, to restrain the instinctive sportiveness of youth, to hush the spirit-song of praise with which, like the awakening bird, she should have welcomed each dawning morn.

'Why must it be thus?' she often asked herself when, restless at midnight as at noon-day, she gazed from her window across the wide star-lit plain, in which groups of melancholy, swaying, pale-hued trees seemed to be whispering secrets of past famine years or sighing weirdly over sorrows to come.

'Will it always be thus?' thought she, 'and is my life to trickle slowly along like the course of our enfeebled stream, until after long assimilation to this desert dreariness I become like one of the house-mothers I see around me? Ignorant, incurious, narrow, with an intelligence gradually shrivelling up to the dimensions of a childhood with which they have nothing else in common! What a hateful prospect! What a death in life to look forward to! Were it not for my darling mother and the few friends I may call my own, I feel as if I could put an end to an existence which has so little to recommend it, so pitiably small an outlook.'

In all this outburst of capricious discontent the experienced reader of the world's page will perceive nothing more than the instinctive, unwarranted impatience of youth, which in man or woman is so utterly devoid of reason or gratitude.

What! does not the vast, calm universe wait and watch, weak railer at destiny, for the completion of 'Nature's wondrous plan,' counting not the years, the æons, as the sands of the sea, that intervene between promise and fulfilment? Hast thou not enjoyed ease, love unwearying, anxious tendance, from the dawn of thy helpless, as yet useless being; and while all creation suffers and travails, canst thou not endure the unfolding of thy fated lot?

Applying, possibly, some such remedies to her mental ailment, life appeared to go on at Corindah much as it had done, Pollie thought, since the earliest days she could remember as a tiny girl. She could almost have supposed that the same things had been said by the same people, or people very like them, since her babyhood. Wonderings whether it would rain soon, by the mildly expectant; doubts whether it would ever rain again, by the scoffers and unbelievers; assertions that the seasons had changed, by the prophets of evil; superficial, sanguine predictions that it would rain some day, by the light-minded; hope and trusting confidence in the Great Ruler, by the devout, that He would not suffer his people to be utterly cast down and forsaken, that the dumb creatures of His hand would have a bound set to their sufferings—all these things had she heard and experienced from time to time ever since she could recall herself as a conscious entity. Then after a less or greater interval the blessed rain of heaven would fall, plenteously, excessively, perhaps superfluously, without warning, without limit, and the long agony of the drought would be over.

Something of this sort had Pollie been saying to her cousin, as they sat at breakfast one gusty, unsettled, red-clouded morning. He had been inquiring satirically whether it ever rained at Corindah.

'He had been here six months and had never seen any. Would all the sheep die? Would all the watercourses dry up? Would they all be forced to abandon the station? And was this a sample of Australia and its vaunted bush life?'

'Things are not quite so bad generally,' laughed Pollie; 'though I cannot deny that in these months, unless the weather changes, it will be what you call a "blue look-out." Poor mother is more anxious every week, and Mr. Gateward's face is becoming fixed in one expression, like that of a bronze idol.'

'It hardly seems like a laughing matter,' said he gravely. 'The loss of the labour of years, of a fortune, and then "Que faire?"'

'I am laughing in faith,' retorted Pollie; 'so that really I am in a more religious frame of mind than all the solemn-faced people who despair of God's goodness. Of course, it will rain some time or other. It might even rain to-night, though it does not look the least like it. Again, it might not rain for a year.'

'What a terribly incomprehensible state of matters to exist in!' said Bertram. 'I little thought, when I grumbled at a rainy week in England, what blessings in disguise I was undervaluing. And what would be the case if a small deluge took place?'

'All the rivers would be in flood. A few shepherds and mail-men, poor fellows! would be drowned, and the whole North-West country, say a thousand miles square, would be one luxuriant prairie of grass nearly as high as your head. Mr. Gateward would sing for joy as far as his musical disabilities would permit him; and poor mother's bank account would be nearly twenty thousand pounds on the right side within a few weeks.'

'And the sheep?'

'A few hundreds would die—the wet and cold would kill them, being weak. All the rest would wax fat, and perhaps kick in a month.'

'Truly wonderful! I must take your word literally, but really I should hardly believe any one else.'

'You may always believe me,' the girl said proudly, as she stood up and faced him, with raised head and erect form, her bright blue eyes fixed steadfastly upon his, and almost emitting a flash, it seemed to him, from their steady glow. 'Promise me that every word I say shall be accepted by you as the absolute, unalterable truth, or I shall speak to you no more about my native land, or anything else.'

'I promise,' he said, taking her hand in his own and reverently bowing over it; 'and now I am going for a long ride, to the outer well; I must be off.'

'To Durbah, forty miles and more?' she said. 'Why did not you make an earlier start? What are you going to ride?'

'Wongamong,' he said. 'He is a wonderful goer, and seems quieter than he was.'

'He is a treacherous, bad-tempered brute,' she returned answer, rather quickly, 'and nothing will ever make him quiet. Besides, I think there's some break of weather coming on. The wind has changed for the third time since sunrise, and the clouds are banking up fast to the west. We might have a storm.'

'What fun!' said the Englishman; 'I should like it of all things. The climate here does not seem to have energy enough for a right down good storm.'

'You don't know what you are talking about,' she said; 'you haven't seen a storm, or a flood, or a bush-fire, or anything. Take my advice and ride a steady horse to-day. Something tells me you might want one. Promise me that you will.'

There was an unusual earnestness in the girl's voice as she spoke, as, placing her hand on his shoulder, she looked in his face. A low muttering roll of thunder seemed to accentuate her appeal. The young man smiled, as he answered, 'My dearest Pollie, I should be sorry to refuse the slightest request so flatteringly in my interest: I will seek me a charger practised in the *ménage* in place of the erratic Wongamong.'

In a few minutes more, as she stood by the open window, she saw him ride through the outer gate on a dark bay horse, whose elastic stride and powerful frame showed him to be one of those rare combinations of strength, speed, and courage, of which the great Australian land holds no inconsiderable number.

'Dear old Guardsman! I'm so glad that he took him. I didn't know that he was in. I wonder what makes me so nervous to-day. It surely cannot be going to *rain*, or is there an earthquake imminent? I believe in presentiments, and if the day is like the others we have had this year, I never shall do so again. There goes another clap of thunder!'

That morning was spent by Pollie Devereux, it must be confessed, in a manner so aimless, so inconsistent with her mother's fixed principles on the score of regular employment for young women, that it drew forth more than one mild reproach from that kindly matron.

'My dear, I can't bear to see you going about from one room to another without settling to anything. Can you not sit down to your work, or practise, or go on with some historical reading, or your French, in which Bertram says you are making such progress? You're wasting your time sadly.'

'Mother!' said her daughter, facing round upon her with mock defiance, 'could you sit down to your work if there was going to be a shipwreck, or a cyclone, or a great battle fought on the plain? Though, really, you good old mother, I think you would, and thread your needle till the Roundheads marched in at the outer gate, as they did in "The Lay of Britomart," or took down the slip-rails, as it would be in our case. But do you know, there is an electrical current in the air, I am sure, and so I, being of a more excitable nature, do really feel so aroused and excited, that I can't keep quiet. Something is going to happen.'

'Now, my dearest Pollie, are not you letting your imagination run away with you? What can happen? There may be a little wind and rain—what the shepherds call "a nice storm"—but nothing else, I fear.'

'"Something wicked this way comes,"' chanted Pollie, putting herself into a dramatic attitude. 'See how dark it is growing! Look at the lightning! Oh, dear, what a flash! And down comes the rain at last—in earnest, too.'

'The rain will have to be very earnest, my dear,' said Mrs. Devereux, 'before poor Corindah feels the benefit of it—though that certainly is a heavy shower. Early in the season too; this is only the 8th of February. There is the lunch-bell. Come along, my dear. A little lunch will do you good.'

'How wet poor Bertram will be!' said Pollie, pityingly. 'He said we couldn't have storms here.'

CHAPTER V

During the half hour bestowed on lunch the weather apparently devoted itself to falsifying Mrs. Devereux's prediction, and raising Pollie to the position of a prophetess. It is a curious fact that in Australia few people are weather-wise. No one can tell, for instance, with any certainty, when it will rain. No one can say with precision when it will not rain. All other forms of weather, be it understood, are immaterial. Rain means everything—peace, plenty, prosperity, the potentiality of boundless wealth; the want of it losses and crosses, sin, suffering, and starvation. For nearly two years the hearts of the dwellers in that vast pastoral region had been made sick with hope deferred. Now, without warning, with no particular indication of change from the long, warm days and still, cloudless nights that seemed as if they would never end, that earth would gradually become desiccated into a grave of all living creatures, suddenly it commenced to rain as if to reproduce the Noachian deluge.

The larger creeks bore a turgid tide, level with their banks, on the surface of which tree-stems and branches, with differing samples of *débris*, whirled floating down.

As the hours passed by with no abatement of violence in the falling of the rain or the fury of the storm, in which the wind had arisen, and raged with tempestuous fury in the darkened sky, a feeling of awe and alarm crept over the minds of the two women.

'There is not a soul about the place, I believe,' said Mrs. Devereux; 'Mr. Gateward is away, and every man and boy with him. During all the years I have been here I have never seen such a storm. Poor Bertram! I hope he has taken shelter somewhere. This cold rain is enough to kill him, with such thin clothing as he has on. But of course he will stay at Baradeen; it would be madness to come on.'

'He said that he would be home to-night, wet or dry. Those were his last words, and he's rather obstinate. Haven't you remarked that, mother?'

'I am afraid he is. It runs in the blood,' the elder remarked, with a sigh. 'But there will be no danger unless the Wawanoo Creek is up. It never rises unless the river does, and there's not rain enough for that.'

'There seems rain enough for anything,' said the girl, shuddering. 'Hark! how it is pouring down now. It will be dark in an hour. I do wish Bertram was home.'

The creek alluded to was a ravine of considerable size and depth, which, serving as one of the anabranches of the river, was rarely filled except in flood time, when it acted as a canal for the purpose of carrying off the superfluous water. Now it was almost dry, and apparently would remain so. It could be distinctly seen from the windows of the room where they were sitting.

At a sudden cry from the girl Mrs. Devereux went to the window. 'What a wonder of wonders!' she said; 'the Wawanoo is coming down. The paling fence in the flat has been carried away.'

The fence alluded to was a high and close palisade across a portion of the flat, down which ran one of the channels of the said Wawanoo Creek. An unusual body of rain, falling apparently during one of the thunder-showers, had completely submerged the valley, which, narrowing above the said fence, and being dammed back by it, finally overbore it, and rushed down the main channel of the creek in a yeasty flood.

'The creek will be twenty feet deep where the road crosses it now,' said Pollie. 'If he comes to it he will have to swim. He will never think of its being so deep, and he might be drowned. I knew something would happen. What a lucky thing he took Guardsman!'

As she spoke her mother pointed to a spot where the track crossed the creek. The road itself was now plainly marked as a sepia-coloured, brown line winding through the grassless, herbless, grey levels of the drought-stricken waste. A horseman was riding at speed along the clearly printed track, through the misty lines of fast-falling rain.

'It is Bertram coming back,' cried Pollie. 'I know Guardsman's long stride; how he is throwing the dirt behind him! I wouldn't mind the ride myself if I had an old habit on. It must be great fun to be as wet as he must be, and to know one cannot be any worse. Do you think he will try to swim the creek?'

'He does not seem to dream of pulling up,' said Mrs. Devereux. 'Very likely he thinks it can't be deep when he crossed dry-shod this morning.'

'Oh, look!' cried the girl, with a long-drawn inspiration. 'He has ridden straight in without stopping. What a plunge! They are both over head and ears in it. But Guardsman swims well. Mr. Gateward told me he saw him in the last flood, when he was only a colt. I can see his head; how he shakes it! Gallant old fellow! And there is Bertram sitting as quietly as if he was on dry land. They will be carried down lower, but it is good shelving land on this side. Now they are out, rather staggering, but safe. Thank God for that! Oh, mother are you not glad?'

As Bertram and the brown made joint entrance to the square opposite the stable-yard, dripping like a sea-horse bestridden by a merman, he saw a feminine figure in the verandah of the barracks gesticulating wildly to him, and in a fashion demanding to be heard.

'Mother says you are to come in directly and change your clothes and take something hot, and not to stay out a moment longer than you can help.'

'I must see Guardsman made snug first,' answered the young man, with the same immovable quiet voice, in which not the slightest inflection betrayed any hint of unusual risk. 'I really couldn't answer it to my conscience to turn him out to-night. I won't be long, however.'

'When it *does* rain here it rains hard, I must admit!' said Mr. Devereux an hour afterwards, as, completely renovated and very carefully attired, he presented himself at dinner. 'Could not have imagined such a transformation scene of earth and sky. The plain has become a gigantic batter pudding, and the ludicrous attempt at a brook—the Wawanoo Creek—is a minor Mississippi. I thought the old horse would have been swept right down once.'

'You will find our rivers and some other Australian matters are not to be laughed at,' answered Pollie, with a heightened colour. 'But mother and I are too glad to see you back safe to scold you for anything you might say to-night.'

'Really I feel quite heroic,' he answered, with a smile which was rarely bestowed with so much kindness; 'I suppose people *are* drowned now and then.'

'I should think so,' said Pollie. 'Do you remember that poor young Clarence, from Amhurst, two or three years ago? He was very anxious to get to the Bindera station, where they were having a party; he was told the creek was dangerous, but would try. His horse got caught in a log or something, and came over with him. He was drowned, and carried into the Bindera house next morning a corpse.'

'Very sad. But men must drop in life's battle now and then. There would be too many of us fellows else "crawling between earth and heaven," as Hamlet says.'

'What a cold-blooded way to talk!' said Pollie; 'but of course you really do not think so. Think of quitting life suddenly with all its pleasures.'

'Pleasures?' replied Mr. Devereux abruptly. 'Yes! I daresay very young persons look at it in that light. After all it's quite a lottery like other games of pitch and toss. Sometimes the backers have it all their own way. Then comes a "fielder's" year, and the first-named are obliterated.'

'Then do you really think life is only another name for a sort of Derby Day on a large scale, or a Grand National?' demanded Pollie, with a shocked expression of countenance—'at the end of which one man is borne in a shining hero, aglow with triumph, while another breaks his neck over the last leap, or loses fame and fortune irrevocably; and that neither can help the appointed lot?'

Her cousin regarded her for a moment with a fixed and searching gaze. Then a ripple of merriment broke over his features, and a rarely seen expression of frank admiration succeeded to the ordinary composure of his visage. 'I don't go quite as far as that.

> "There's a divinity that shapes our ends,
> Rough-hew them how we will."

But I am afraid few of us live as if we thought so. That ever I should have found myself in Australia was at one time so unlikely, so all but impossible, that I may well believe in the interposition of a Ruler of Events.'

———————————

'I believe they've had rain,' is the usual answer to him who 'speirs' in Australia as to the pastoral welfare of a particular province, district, or locality. It is unnecessary to say more. 'Man wants but little here below' is comparatively true; but a short supply of the aqueous fluid on land parallels in its destructive effects the over abundance at sea. When the rain is withheld for a year or two years, as the case may be, losses accumulate, and ruin stalks on apace. The severity of the acknowledged droughts, not merely accidental drynesses, is comparative, and is often matter of conversation.

'This is the worst drought known for many years,' was remarked to a young but war-worn pioneer.

'Pretty well, but not equal to that of 187-,' he made answer.

'Why do you think so?'

'When that drought commenced,' he said slowly, 'we had nine thousand head of cattle on our run on the Darwin. When it broke up we mustered sixteen hundred, and on foot too: we had not had a horse to ride for eighteen months.'

From such merciless disaster was Corindah now saved. Prosperity was assured for at least two years, as well to that spacious property which comprehended 290,000 acres (and not a bad one among them, as Mr. Gateward was fond of asserting) as to a hundred similar pastoral leaseholds from the Macquarie to the Darr. An entirely new state of matters had suddenly arisen. In all directions telegraphic messages were speeding through space, withdrawing this lot of 20,000 ewes or that of a thousand store bullocks from sale; while eager forecasting operators like Mr. Jack Charteris had swept up the supply of saleable sheep, and left their more cautious comrades lamenting their inability to purchase except at prices which 'left no margin,' the alternative being to have tens of thousands of acres of waving prairie 'going to waste' for want of stock to eat it. The face of Nature had indeed changed. Within a fortnight the arid dusty plains, so barren of aspect, were carpeted with a green mantle, wondrously vivid of hue and rapid of growth. The creek ran musically murmuring towards the river, which itself 'came down,' a tawny, turbid stream bank high, and in places overflowing into long dry lagoons and lakelets. Even the birds of the air seemed to be apprised of the wondrous atmospheric change. Great flocks of wild-fowl soared in, migrating from undreamed of central wastes. The lakelets and the river reaches were alive with the heron and the egret. The bird of the wilderness, with giant beak and sweeping wing, was there in battalions; while the roar of wings when a cloud of wild-fowl rose from water was like a discharge of artillery.

Bertram Devereux was, in his heart, truly astonished at the wondrous change wrought in the outward appearance of the region, in the manner and bearing of the dwellers therein, in the tone of the leading newspapers, in everybody's plans, position, and prospects, which had been wrought by so simple and natural an agent. He, however, carefully preserved his ordinary incurious, impassive immobility, and after casually remarking that this was evidently one of the lands known to the author of the *Arabian Nights*, and that somebody had been rubbing the magic lamp, and commanded a genie to fetch a few million tons of water from Ireland or Upper India, where it was superfluous, and deliver it here, made no other observation, but rode daily with Mr. Gateward over the sodden, springing pastures, wading through the overflowing marshes, and swimming the dangerous creeks 'where ford there was none,' as if he had always expected the West Logan to be akin to the west of Ireland as to soil and climate, and was not disappointed in his expectation.

On the morning after the flood Harold Atherstone had betaken himself to the metropolis, only to be forestalled by Jack Charteris in his rapid and comprehensive purchases of stock. Doubtless other pastoral personages had been duly informed by the magic wire of the momentous change, but even then, such had been the terror, the suffering, the dire endurance of every evil of a twofold ruin, that numbers of owners were found willing to sell their advertised sheep at a very slight advance upon the pre-pluvial prices. So might they be assured of the solvency and security which they had dreaded would never be theirs again. So might they again lay their heads on their pillow at night, thanking God for all His mercies, and for the safety of the future of those dear to them. So might they again be enabled to go forth among their fellow-men, strong in the consciousness that the aching dread, the long-deferred hope, the dark despair slowly creeping on like some dimly seen but implacable beast of prey, were things of the past, phantoms and shadows to be banished for ever from their unhaunted lives.

All these but lately altered circumstances were distinctly in favour of a quick and decisive operator, as was Harold Atherstone when he 'saw his way.' Not a plunger like Jack Charteris, he was firm and rapid of evolution when he had distinctly demonstrated his course of action. So when he returned to Maroobil after a month's absence, he had as many sheep on the road, at highly paying prices, as would keep that 'well-known fattening station' and Corindah besides in grass-eaters for many a month to come. Mrs. Devereux was full of gratitude towards him for managing her delegated business so safely and promptly, and again and again declared that there was no living man like Harold Atherstone. He was always to be relied on in the hour of need. He never made mistakes, or was taken in, or forgot things, or procrastinated, like other men. When he said he would do a thing, that thing was done, if it was in the compass of mortal man to do it.

'In short,' said Pollie, before whom and for whose benefit and edification this effusive statement was made, 'in short, he is perfection—a man without a fault. What a pity it is that paragons are never attractive!'

'Beware of false fires, my darling,' said the tender mother—'misleading lights of feeling apart from reason, which are apt to wreck the trusting, and to end in despairing darkness.'

Among the visitors to Corindah, who made at least a bi-monthly call, was the Honourable Hector MacCallum, M.L.C.

He was a prosperous bachelor, verging on middle age, with several good stations, and an enviable power of leaving them in charge of managers and overseers, while he disported himself in the pleasantest spots of the adjacent colonies, or indeed wheresoever he listed—sometimes even in Tasmania, where he was famed for his picnics, four-in-hand driving, and liberality in entertaining. In that favoured isle, where maidens fair do so greatly preponderate, Mr. MacCallum might have brought back a wife from any of his summer trips; and few would have asserted that the damsel honoured by his choice was other than among the fairest and sweetest of that rose-garden of girls.

But then something always prevented him. He wanted to go to New Zealand. It was impossible to settle down before he had seen the wonders of that wonderland—the pink-and-white terraces, the geysers, the paradisiacal gardens, the Eves that flitted through the 'rata' thickets, the fountains that dripped and flashed through the hush of midnight. Something was always incomplete. He would come again. And more than one fair cheek grew pale, and bright eyes lost their lustre, ere the inconstant squatter prince was heralded anew.

But now it seemed as if the goodly fish, which had so often drawn back and disappeared, was about to take the bait.

Mr. MacCallum's visits were apparently accidental. He happened to be in that part of the country, and took the opportunity of calling. He was on his way to Melbourne or Sydney, and was sure he could execute a commission for Mrs. Devereux or Miss Pollie. This, of course, involved a visit on the way back. He was a good-looking, well-preserved man, so that his forty odd years did not put him at much disadvantage, if any, when he came into competition with younger men. Indeed, it is asserted by the experienced personages of their own sex that young girls are in general not given to undervalue the attentions of men older than themselves. It flatters their vanity or gratifies their self-esteem to discover that their callow charms and undeveloped intellects, so lately emancipated from the prosaic thraldom of the schoolroom, suffice to attract men who have seen the world—have, perhaps, borne themselves 'manful under shield' in the battlefield of life, have struck hard in grim conflicts where quarter is neither given nor received, and been a portion of the great 'passion-play' of the universe. They look down upon their youthful admirers as comparatively raw and inexperienced, like themselves. Theirs is a career of hope and expectation all to come, like their own. They like and esteem them, perhaps take their parts in rehearsals of the old, old melodrama. But in many cases it is not till they see at their feet the war-worn soldier, the scarred veteran who has tempted fate so often in the great hazards of the campaign, who has shared the cruel privations, the deadly hazards of real life —that the imaginative heart of woman fills up all the spaces in the long-outlined sketch of the hero and the king, the lord and master of her destiny, to whom she is henceforth proud to yield worship and loving service.

Why Mr. MacCallum did not marry all this time—he owned to thirty-seven, and his enemies said he was more like forty-five—the dwellers in the country towns on the line of march exhausted themselves in conjecturing. The boldest hazarded the guess that he might have an unacknowledged wife 'at home.' Others averred that he was pleasure-loving, of epicurean, self-indulgent tastes, having neither high ambition nor religious views. They would be sorry to trust Angelina or Frederica to such a guardianship. Besides, he was getting quite old. In a few years there would be a great change in him. He had aged a good deal since that last trip of his to Europe, when he had the fever in Rome. Of course he was wealthy, but money was not everything, and a man who spent the greater part of the year at his club was not likely to make a particularly good husband.

The object of all this criticism, comment, and secret exasperation was a squarely built, well-dressed man, slightly above the middle height, and with that indefinable ease of manner and social tact that travel, leisure, and the possession of an assured position generally produce. He was kindly, amusing, invariably polite, and deferential to women of all ages; and there were few who did not acknowledge the charm of his manner, even when they abused him in his absence, or deceived him for their own purposes. In spite of all he was popular, was the Honourable Hector, a man of wide and varied experience, of a bearing and general *tournure* which left little to be desired. In the matter of courtship he knew sufficiently well that it was injudicious to force the running; that a waiting race was his best chance. He took care never to prolong his visit; always to encircle himself with some surrounding of interest during his stay at Corindah. He pleased Pollie and her mother by being in possession of the newest information on all subjects in which he knew they were interested. He was good-natured and *bon camarade* with the young men, at the same time in a quiet way exhibiting a slight superiority—as of one whose sphere was larger, whose possessions, interests, opportunities, and prospects generally, placed him upon a different plane from that with which the ordinary individual must be contented. This, of course, rendered more effective the habitual deference which he invariably yielded to both the ladies whom he wished to propitiate, rightly deeming that all the avenues to Pollie's heart were guarded by the mental presentment of her mother.

'Really, we quite miss Mr. MacCallum when he leaves Corindah,' said Pollie one day, as she watched the well-appointed mail-phaeton and high-bred horses which that gentleman always affected, disappearing in the distance. 'He's most amusing and well-informed; his manners are so finished—really, there is hardly anything about him that you could wish altered.'

'So clever and practical, too, said Mrs. Devereux. 'He showed me in a few minutes how he was going to lay out the garden at the new house at Wanwondah. Really, it will be the most lovely place. And the irrigation is from a plan of his own.'

'It's almost a pity to be so extravagant there, isn't it?' said her daughter. 'He told me he never saw it except in the winter and spring. He always spends the summer in some other colony. This year he will go to the hot springs of

Waiwera, and see all that delicious North Island, and those unutterably lovely pink-and-white terraces. How I should like to go!'

'Quite easy,' said Harold Atherstone, who had been standing by the mantlepiece apparently in a fit of abstraction. 'You've to say "yes" to the Honourable Hector's unspoken prayer, and he'll take you there, or to the moon, when Mr. Cook discovers a practicable route. He's not more than twenty years older than you are—hardly that.'

'So you think I am likely to marry for the new house at Wanwondah Crossing-place?' retorted Pollie. 'Also for the power of going away and leaving all you stupid people to be roasted and boiled during the long dismal summer? Poor things! what would you do without me to tease you all? But it's a strange peculiarity of society, I believe, that a girl can never make any personal remark but invariably the next idea suggested to her by her friends is, "Whom is she trying to marry?" That being so, why shouldn't I marry Mr. MacCallum? Not that he has ever asked me.'

'But he will—you know he will—and if you allow yourself to be carried away by dreams of luxury and unlimited power of travel, which is more likely, you will regret it once only—that is, all your life after.'

'But say you are not serious, my darling,' said her mother, with a half-alarmed look. 'Really, I will take you to Tasmania, or even New Zealand, though it's dreadfully rough—anywhere, rather than you should be tempted to act against your better judgment. Mr. MacCallum is extremely nice and suitable—but he is far too *old* for you.'

'I don't see that at all,' replied the young lady petulantly. 'I like some one I can look up to. All women do. He knows the world of society, letters, politics —not only of these colonies either. Most other girls would—perhaps the phrase is vulgar—"jump at him." Besides, he is most amusing. Not a mere talker, but full of crisp, pleasant expressions and suggestions. He is a new magazine, with the leaves uncut. Not like some people, gloomy and abstracted half the time.'

'You don't see *him* when he's off colour—excuse my slang,' answered the young man. 'He is not always amusing, people say. But that's not my affair. If age and experience are the valued qualities, I'm sorry I was not born a generation earlier. And now I must say good-bye; I'm wanted at the back-block Inferno, and have no idea when I shall see you again.'

'If you are not here this day fortnight,' said the young lady, with a solemn and tragic expression, 'and at tea-time, see to it.'

'But there's all sorts of trouble at Ban Ban. The dogs are showing up. All the sheep have to come in. There are no shepherds to be got. My working overseer is laid up with acute rheumatism. How can I——'

'Shepherd or no shepherd,' persisted the girl,—'rain or shine—rheumatism or not—this day fortnight, or you will take the consequence.'

'I suppose I must manage it,' quoth the unfortunate young man. 'Do you remember your *Ivanhoe*: "Gurth, the son of Beowulf, is the born thrall of Cedric of Rotherwood"? Seems to me that villenage is not extinct, even in this colonial and democratic community.'

'And a very good thing too,' retorts this haughty, undisciplined damsel. 'The feudal system had an amazing deal of good about it. I don't see why we shouldn't revive it out here.'

'Looks rather it at present!' grumbled Harold. 'Good-bye, Mrs. Devereux. Fortunately the rain's general, so we can stand a good deal of oppression and intimidation.'

'In the spring a young man's fancy lightly turns to thoughts of love,'

sang the laureate. And the parallel is sound. Of course it always rains in spring in England.

But suppose it didn't—as in Australia? He would find that things went differently. The 'wanton lapwing' would not get himself another crest, and the poet would have to furnish himself with another example.

In the absence of rain we can assure our readers that things are much otherwise, even with the dumb and feathered tribes. The wild-fowl do come down in a serious, philosophical sort of way. But what they do in effect is this:—

They say—'We have ciphered this thing out, and have come to the conclusion that it is not going to rain, that it will be a dry spring. That being the case, we are not going to pair, or build, or lay eggs, or going through the ordinary foolishness, in anticipation of rain and certain other adjuncts to matrimony, which *will not come*.

And they do *not* pair.

How are such things managed? Who teaches the birds of the air? How do they know it is going to keep dry?

Yet the results are as I state. There is no young family to provide for, no presents, no trousseaux—and a very good thing, too, under the circumstances.

So with the social and amatory enterprises of the human inhabitants of the dry country; the phenomenon of six inches of rain or otherwise makes all the difference. Mr. Oldhand had promised to build his youngest son Dick a new cottage at the Bree Bree station, which he had managed for him successfully for several years, after which Dick's marriage with Mary Newcome was to take place, they having been engaged, as was well known to the neighbours here, for the last three years. But the season 'set in dry.' Dick had a bad lambing, and lost sheep besides. So the cottage can't be built this year, the marriage is put off, and Dick's manly countenance wears an air of settled gloom.

Ergo, it follows that immediately upon the supervening of a period of unexampled prosperity, consequent upon the abnormal rainfall which 'ran' Wawanoo Creek in half an hour, and narrowly escaped devoting Bertram Devereux to the unappeased deities of the waste as a befitting sacrifice, proposals of marriage were thick in the air, and matrimonial offers became nearly as plentiful as bids for store sheep.

When Hector MacCallum therefore, as became him, gallantly took the lead as representative of the marrying pastoral section, no one wondered. Speculation and conjecture doubtless, were evoked as to where the many-stationed Sultan might deign to cast his coveted kerchief. In despite of inter-provincial jealousies, however, no one was much astonished when reliable information was disseminated to the effect that he had been on a visit of nearly a week to Corindah, had been seen driving Mrs. and Miss Devereux to points of interest in the neighbourhood in his mail-phaeton, that his groom's livery was more resplendent than ever, and that the famous chestnuts had been replaced by a team of brown horses, admirably matched, thorough-bred, and said to be the most valuable turn-out in work on this side of the line. Acidulated persons, as usual, made exclamation to the effect that 'they never could see what there was in that girl; some people had wonderful luck; boldness and assurance seemed to take better than any other qualities with the men nowadays,' and so on. But when gradually it oozed out that there was no triumphant proclamation of engagement after all, that Mr. MacCallum was going to England, could not be back for two or three years, etc.—all of which certainly pointed to the fact of his proposals having been declined, impossible as such a fact would appear—the clamour of the hard-to-please contingent rose loud and high. 'What did the girl want? Was she waiting for a prince of the blood? After having befooled all the men within her reach, from Jack Charteris to the parson, and ending up with a man old enough to be her father, and who certainly should have known better, was it not heartless and indecent to treat him as she had done? Would not the whole district cry shame upon her, and she be left lamenting in a few years, deserted by every one that had any sense? A vinegary old maid in the future—it would be all her own fault, and that of her mother's ridiculous vanity and indulgence.'

All unknowing or careless of these arrows of criticism, the free and fearless maiden pursued her career. Mr. MacCallum had, at a well-chosen moment, made his effort and pressed with practised persistence for a favourable answer. But in vain. Under other conditions, men of his age and attributes have been frequently successful, to the wrath and astonishment of younger rivals. But circumstances have been in their favour. Poverty, ignorance of the world, ambition on the part of the girl's friends, gratitude, have all or each conspired in such case to turn the scale in favour of the wealthy and adroit, if mature, wooer. And so the contract, often a fairly happy one, is concluded.

But in this case Love, the lord of all, had fair play for once. Pollie had distinctly made up her mind, since she was conscious of possessing such a faculty, that she would never marry any one unless she was in love with him ardently, passionately, romantically, without any manner of doubt. People might come and try to please. She could not help that. It was hardly in her nature to be cold or rude to anybody. But as to marrying any one she only liked, she would die first.

She liked, she respected, she in every way approved of Mr. MacCallum; but no! She was much honoured, flattered, and pleased, and really shrank from the idea of giving him so much pain. Mr. MacCallum exaggerated his probable agonies in such a way that a weaker woman might probably have given in—from sheer pity. But as to marrying him, it was out of the question. Her answer was 'No,' and nothing could ever alter it.

So the Honourable Hector had to depart in a more disappointed and disgusted frame of mind than had happened to His Royal Highness for many a day. Drought, debts, dingoes, travelling sheep, were all as nothing to this crowning disaster. Everything else being so flourishing, it was a thunderbolt out of a blue sky, crushing his equanimity and self-satisfaction to the dust.

Not his happiness, however. A middle-aged bachelor with a good digestion and enviable bank balance is not—whatever the sensational novelist may assert—usually slaughtered by one such miscalculation. He does not like it, of course. He fumes and frets for a week or two, and probably says, 'Confound the girl! I thought she really liked me.' Then he falls back upon the time-honoured calculation—a most arithmetically correct one—of those 'other fish in the sea.' Claret has a soothing effect. The Club produces alleviating symptoms. And the Laird of Cockpen either marries the next young lady on his list, or, departing to far lands, discovers that the supply of Calypsos and

Ariadnes is practically unlimited.

MacCallum, like a shrewd personage, as he was, held his tongue and took the next mail for Europe, reappearing within two years with an exceedingly handsome and lady-like wife, who did full justice to his many good qualities, was very popular, and made Wanwondah quite the show country-house of the neighbourhood.

CHAPTER VI

After this stupendous incident had ruffled the waters of provincial repose, a long untroubled calm succeeded. Little was heard in the article of news except the weekly chronicle of stock movements: who had sold, who had bought, who, having stocked up—that is, filled his run with all the sheep it would carry, and more—had sold to a new arrival, and gone to England 'for good,' or at least till the long-dated station bills became due. Among this last-named division was Mr. Jack Charteris, who, having sold one of his far-out runs to a Queenslander, considered this to be a favourable opportunity to take 'a run home,' as he expressed it, for a year, for various specified reasons which he displayed before his friends, such as seeing the world and renewing his constitution, lately injured by hard work and anxiety. So he ostentatiously took his passage by a well-known mail-steamer, and made all ready to start in a couple of months. He had, however, two plans *in petto*, of which he did not advise society generally.

One was, by personal application to English capitalists—being provided with all proper credentials from his bankers and others, with a carefully drawn out schedule of his properties (purchased lands, leasehold, sheep, cattle, horses, outside country), with carefully kept accounts showing the profits upon stations and stock for the last five or ten years, the increasing value of the wool clip, and the annual expenditure upon permanent improvements; the whole with personal valuation (approximate), and references to leading colonists of rank and position—to discover whether he, John Charteris, with an improving property, but constantly in want of cash advances, could not secure a loan for a term of years at English rates of interest, say five or six per cent, instead of at colonial rates, eight, nine, and ten. This would make a considerable difference to Mr. Jack's annual disbursements, relieve him from anxiety when the money-market hardened, and would, moreover, euchre his friends the bankers in Sydney, with whom he was wont to carry on a half-playful, half-serious war of words whenever they met.

His other *coup* was to make a farewell visit to Corindah, and at the last moment 'try his luck,' as he phrased it, with the daughter of the house. He was not over sanguine, but in reviewing the situation, he decided that with women, as with other 'enterprises of great pith and moment,' you never know what you can do till you try. He ran over all the reasons for and against on his fingers—as he was wont to do in a bargain for stock—finally deciding that he would 'submit an offer.'

Many a time and often had he acted similarly after the same calculation—

offered a price far below the owner's presumable valuation and the market rate of the article. As often, to his great surprise, it had been accepted. He would do so now.

'Let me see,' he said to himself. 'Old MacCallum got the sack, they say. I rather wonder at that—that is, I should have wondered if it had been any other girl. Not another girl in the district but would have accepted him on his knees. Such a house—such horses! Good-looking, pleasant fellow, full-mouthed of course, but sound on his pins, hardly a grey hair—regular short price in the betting. What a sell for him! Well, now about Jack Charteris. How stands he for odds? Nine-and-twenty next birthday; fairly good-looking, so the girls say; plenty of pluck, good nature, and impudence; ride, run, shoot, or fight any man of his weight in the country. Clever? Well, I wish I was a little better up in those confounded books. If I were, I really believe I might go in and win. The only man I'm afraid of is that confounded cousin fellow. He is infernally sly and quiet, and, I expect, is coming up in the inside running. I'd like to punch his head.'

Here Mr. Charteris stood up, squared his shoulders, and delivered an imaginary right and left into an enemy with extraordinary gusto. Then exclaiming, 'Here goes anyhow! I'll go in for it on my way to Sydney. I'll provide a retreat in case of total rout and defeat. It will be half forgotten by the time I return.'

To resolve and to execute were with Mr. Charteris almost simultaneous acts. Working night and day until his preparations were complete, he sent on a note to say when he might be expected, and on the appointed evening drove up, serious and determined, to Corindah gate. He was received with so much cordiality that he half thought his mission was accomplished, and that the princess would accompany him to Europe without notice, which would have been one of the rapid and triumphant *coups* in which his speculative soul delighted. The real reason was, that both ladies were moved in their feminine hearts by the idea of so old an acquaintance going a journey to a far land, and were sensitively anxious to show him all the honour and attention they could under such exceptional circumstances.

So the best of us are deceived occasionally. Who has not seen the unwonted sparkle in a woman's eyes and as often as not—if the truth be told—put a totally wrong interpretation upon the signal?

Thus Mr. Charteris fared, much encouraged, and greatly heightened in determination. He was at his best and brightest all the evening, and when he said—pressing Pollie's hand as they parted—that he wanted to say a last word to her about his voyage if she would be in the orangery before breakfast, that young woman assented in the most unsuspicious manner, believing it to be something about Maltese lace, as to which she had given him a most unmerciful commission. So, shaking his hand with renewed fervour, she went off to bed, leaving Mr. Charteris in the seventh heaven, and almost unable to sleep for the tumultuous nature of his emotions.

The sun was closely inspected by John Charteris next morning, from its earliest appearance until after about an hour's radiance had been shed upon the vast ocean of verdure, from which its heat extracted a silvery mist. How different from the outlook one little year ago! His eye roamed over the vast expanse meditatively, as if calculating the number of sheep to the acre such a grass crop would sustain, if one could only have it for five years all the season through. Suddenly he became aware of a light form flitting through the dark-green foliage and gold-globed greenery of the orangery.

In a moment he was by her side. His face lit up with innocent pleasure as she greeted him with childish joy. In her heart she thought she had never known him so pleasant in his manner, so nice and friendly, and yet reticent, before. If so improved now, what would he be when he returned from Europe? She had no more idea of any *arrière pensée* in meeting him by appointment in the garden than if he had been the Bishop of Riverina.

When Mr. Charteris, after a few unconnected remarks about the beauty of the weather, the prospects of the season, his sorrow for leaving all his old friends, thought it time to come to the point, especially as Pollie in the goodness of her heart replied to the last statement with 'Not more sorry than they are to lose you, Mr. Charteris,' he certainly produced an effect.

'Oh, Miss Devereux, oh, my dearest Pollie, if you will let me call you so, why should we part at all? Surely you must see the affection I've cherished, the feelings I've had for you ever since we first met. Years and years I've stood by and said nothing, because—because I was doubtful of your affection, but now, now!'

Here he took her hand and began gently to draw her towards him, putting an imploring expression into his eyes, which was so utterly foreign to their usual merry and audacious expression, that Pollie, after one wild, fixed gaze of horrified anxiety, as if to see whether he had not become suddenly insane, burst into a fit of uncontrollable laughter.

'Miss Devereux, surely,' began he, with a hurt and surprised look, 'this is not exactly fair or kind under the circumstances. What I have said may or may not be ridiculous, but it is generally looked upon as a compliment paid to a young lady and not as a matter, pardon me, for ridicule and contempt.'

The girl's face changed suddenly. She made a strong effort and prevented herself from lapsing into what might have been an hysterical outbreak of mirth.

'Mr. Charteris,' she said gravely, 'I am the last person, as you ought to know, likely to hurt your feelings consciously; but I might ask you whether you think it right or fair to entice me here, with my mind running on Maltese lace and Cingalese ornaments, which were the last things we spoke about last night, and suddenly fire off a proposal in form at me. I declare I was never more astonished in my life. Whatever could you be thinking of?'

'What every one who sees you is thinking of,' answered Jack, humbly and regretfully—'love and admiration for your sweet self. Oh! Miss Devereux, I worship the very ground you stand upon.'

'I will never be decently civil to any one again,' declared Pollie. 'I suppose you saw mother and I were glad to see you, and so thought—Heaven forgive you!—that I had fallen in love with you. Don't you know that girls never show their feelings that way? It will be a lesson to you another time. Don't say another word. We shall always be good friends, I hope. When you come out with a wife—you'll find lots of nicer girls than me in England, so everybody says—we shall laugh over this. Mother and I will hold our tongues; nobody need know. I shall not show at breakfast. You had better tell her, and she will comfort you. Good-bye.'

She looked him frankly in the face and held out her hand, which poor Jack took ruefully, and raising it to his lips, turned away. When he looked round, she had disappeared. The glory of the morning had passed away with her. He made a melancholy attempt to whistle, and slowly betook himself to the stables, where he arranged that his luggage should be stowed in his phaeton and all things made ready for a start at a moment's notice after breakfast.

This done, he sauntered into the house, and, intercepting Mrs. Devereux before she reached the breakfast-room, told her of the melancholy occurrence with a countenance to match, and begged her pardon and her daughter's for making so great a mistake.

Mrs. Devereux was a tender-hearted woman, and, as are most of her age, inclined to condone all offences of this nature, though, like her daughter, as Mr. Charteris resentfully felt, she expressed extreme astonishment at the idea of his having come with malice prepense to make so serious a proposition. She was sure that Pollie had not given him reason to think that she had any other feeling for him but that of sincere, unalloyed friendship, which they had always felt, and, she trusted, always would.

But Mr. Charteris' humility broke down and changed at this point into something very like a strong sense of unfair treatment. 'Confound it!' he broke out. 'That is, I beg a thousand pardons; but it appears to me the first time in my life that you are not quite just, Mrs. Devereux. How in the world is a man to find out if a girl likes him, if he doesn't ask her? Is he to wait years and years until they both grow old, or until he worries her into making some sign that she cares for him more than other fellows? I call that rather a mean way. I must say I thought Miss Devereux liked me, and that's enough in my mind for a man to begin on. I've had my shot, and missed. But for the life of me, I can't see where I've acted either unlike a man or a gentleman.'

As Jack stood straight up and delivered himself of this explanation of his views and principles, with a heightened colour and a kindling eye, Mrs. Devereux could not help thinking that he would have advanced his views very much with her daughter if he had spoken to her in the same decided tone and manner. 'He really is a fine young man,' she thought to herself, 'and very good-looking too. But there's no persuading a wilful girl. I hope she may never do worse.'

Then she took Jack's hand herself in her's, and said, 'My dear John, neither I nor Polly would hurt your feelings for the world. It *did* take us by surprise; but perhaps I ought to have noticed that your admiration for her was genuine. I quite agree with you that it is more manly and straightforward for a man to declare himself positively. I am sure we shall always look upon you as one of our best and dearest friends.'

'I hope Miss Pollie may do better,' said Jack gloomily, as he pressed the hand of the kind matron. 'She may or she may not. A girl doesn't always judge men rightly until it is too late—too late—but whether or no, God bless her and you in that and everything else! Don't forget poor Jack Charteris.'

And he was gone.

Mr. Charteris, with habitual forethought, had left nothing till the last moment. As he came into the yard, he had but to take the reins and gain the box-seat. His horses plunged at their collars, and swept out of the yard across the plain at a rate which showed that they were instinctively aware that a rapid start was intended. Half-way across the first plain he encountered Harold Atherstone on horseback, looking like a man who had already had a long ride.

'Hallo! Jack, whither away? You look as if you were driving against time. What's up?'

'Well, I'm off by next week's mail-steamer, as I told you before. I've been at Corindah since yesterday, where I've been fool enough to run my head against a post. I needn't explain.' Harold nodded sympathetically. 'We're in the same boat, I expect. I wouldn't care if you were the fortunate man, old fellow; though every one has a right to try his own luck. But I expect we shall both be euchred by that infernal, smooth-faced, mild-voiced, new-chum cousin. I can't see what there is to attract the women about him; but they are all in the same line. I heard Bella Pemberton praising him up hill and down dale. I suppose there is a fate in these things. Where is he now?'

'I am not prepared to agree with all you say,' answered Harold calmly. 'The end will show. I don't trust him too much myself, though I should be puzzled upon what to ground my "Doctor Fell" feeling. He is away on some back country that Mrs. Devereux has rented, and won't be back for a month.'

'I hope his horse will put its foot in a crab-hole and break its neck,' said Jack viciously. 'I wouldn't mind the girl being carried away from us by a *man*. She has a right to follow her fancy. But a pale-faced, half-baked, sea-sick looking beggar like that—it's more than a fellow can bear.'

'Come, Jack, you're unjust, and not over respectful to Miss Devereux herself. But I make allowances. Good-bye, old man. *Bon voyage!* Bring out a rosy-cheeked English girl. Hearts are reparable commodities, you know. Yours has been broken before.'

'Never like this, Harold; give you my word. I could sell the whole place, and cut the colony for ever, I feel so miserable and downhearted. But I'm not one of the lie-down-and-die sort, so I suppose I shall risk another entry. Good-bye, old man. God bless you!'

A silent hand-grasp, and the friends parted. Mr. Charteris' equipage gradually faded away in the mirage of the far distance, while Harold rode quietly onward towards his own station—much musing and with a heart less calm than his words had indicated.

When he arrived at the spot where the tracks diverged, he was conscious of a strong instinctive inclination—first of his steed, and then of himself—to take the track which led to Corindah. After combating this not wholly logical tendency, and telling himself that it was his first duty to go and see that all things were well in order at home before making his usual call at Corindah, he descried another horseman coming rather fast across the plain, and evidently making for the Corindah track.

Pulling up so as to give the stranger an opportunity for ranging alongside, he presently said to himself involuntarily, 'Why, it's the parson; and furthermore, I shall have to go to Corindah now, as the old lady says she finds it hard work entertaining Courtenay all by himself. He's not a bad hand at talking, but he's so terrifically serious and matter-of-fact that he's rather much for a couple of women. When Bertram's there it's better, for I notice he generally contrives to get up an argument with him, and bowl him over on some point of church history. That fellow Bertram knows everything, to do him justice.'

As these thoughts passed through his mind the individual referred to cantered up on an active-looking hackney, rather high in bone, and greeted him with pleased recognition.

'I was debating in my own mind, Mr. Atherstone,' he said, 'whether I should hold divine service at your station to-day or at that of Mrs. Devereux.'

'You are equally welcome at both houses, as you know,' said the layman; 'but I think it may be perhaps a more convenient arrangement in all respects to manage it in this way. If you will ride home with me now to Maroobil, I will see that all the men are mustered and the wool-shed got ready to-night. I can send a messenger to Corindah with a note telling Mrs. Devereux that you and I will be there to-morrow night, which will be Saturday. She will then have everything prepared for a regular morning service on Sunday.'

The clergyman bowed assentingly. 'I think that will suit better than the plan I had proposed to myself of going there to-night. There are a good many people within a few hours' ride of Corindah, and Mrs. Devereux always kindly sends word to them of my arrival. The Sabbath will be the more appropriate day for divine service at Corindah, where there will probably be a larger gathering.'

'Then we may as well ride,' said the other, looking at his watch, 'and we shall be in time for a late lunch at Maroobil.'

The Rev. Cyril Courtenay was a spare, rather angular young man, about seven-and-twenty, who had a parish about as large as Scotland to supply, as he best might, with religious nourishment and spiritual consolation. He had taken a colonial University degree, and was therefore well instructed in a general way, in addition to which he was a gentleman by birth and early training. He was gifted with a commendable amount of zeal for the cause of true religion generally, if more particularly for the Church of England, of which he was an ordained clergyman.

His duties were different from what they would have been in an English parish. The distances were indeed magnificent. His stipend was paid chiefly by the voluntary contributions of the inhabitants of the district of West Logan, and partly from a fund of which the bishop of his diocese had the management, and from which he was able to supplement the incomes of the poorer clergy. This amounted to about two hundred and fifty pounds per annum. The contributories were almost entirely squatters. The other laymen of the denomination—labourers, shepherds, station hands, boundary riders, etc.—though they attended his services cheerfully, did not consider themselves bound to pay anything; holding, apparently, that the Rev. Cyril was included in the category of 'swells'—a class radically differing from themselves, whose subsistence was safe and assured, being provided for in some mysterious manner between the squatters and the Government, by whom all the good things of this life, in their opinion, including 'place and pay,' were distributed at will.

The horse of the Rev. Cyril had started off when Mr. Atherstone gave the signal to his own hackney, and powdered along the level road as if a hand-gallop was the only pace with which he was acquainted. It is a curious fact that the clergymen of all Protestant denominations ride hard, and are not famous for keeping their horses in good condition. *Exceptis excipiendis*, of course. There are not many of them, either, to whom the laity are anxious to lend superior hackneys. They are accused, and not without reason, of being hard on their borrowed mounts, and of not being careful of their sustenance. The priest of the Romish communion, on the other hand, invariably has a good horse, in good condition. He treats him well and tenderly withal. Why this difference? Why the balance of care and merciful dealing on the side of our Roman Catholic brethren? For one thing, priests are chiefly Irishmen, who are horsemen and horse-lovers to a man. Then the celibate Levite, having no human outlet for his affections, pets his steed, as the old maid her cat. With the married clergyman the oats of the rough-coated, though serviceable, steed come often in competition with the butcher's and baker's bills or the children's schooling. The married parson's horse, like himself, must work hard on the smallest modicum of sustenance, lodging, and support that will keep body and soul together. And very good work the pair often do.

The Rev. Cyril, however, being a bachelor, and living a good deal at free quarters, was not an impecunious individual. He should therefore have had his hackney in better order. But it was more a matter of carelessness with him than lack of purpose. He had not been a horseman in his youth. Australian born as he was, he had studied hard and permitted himself few recreations of a physical kind; so that when, after serving as a catechist, he was appointed to the district of West Logan, where he had two or three hundred miles a week to ride or drive in a general way, he found himself awkwardly deficient in this particular accomplishment.

To take a man-servant with him always would have doubled his expenses, without being of any corresponding benefit. After trying it for a few months he gave it up. He then took to riding and driving himself—at first with partial success, inasmuch as he had several falls, and the periodical overthrow of the parson's buggy became part of the monthly news of the district. Gradually, however, he attained to that measure of proficiency which enables a man to ride a quiet horse along a road or through open country, besides being able to drive a buggy without colliding with obstacles. He certainly drove with painfully loose reins, and rode his horse much after the sailor's fashion, as if they are warranted to go fifty miles without stopping. However, he got on pretty well on the whole, and Australian horses, like Cossack ponies, being accustomed to stand a good deal of violent exercise with the aid only of occasional feeding and no grooming at all, Mr. Courtenay and his steed got through their work and adventures reasonably well.

Three o'clock saw the two young men at the Maroobil home station, a large, old-fashioned, comfortable congeries of buildings, without attempt at architectural embellishment. The barns, sheds, and stables were massive and commodious, showing signs of having been built in that earlier period of colonial history when less attention was paid to rapidity of construction. The garden was full of fruit-trees of great age and size, which even in the late droughts seemed to have been supplied with adequate moisture. Comfort and massiveness had been the leading characteristics of the establishment since its foundation. Homesteads have a recognisable expression at first sight, even as their proprietors.

A neat brown-faced groom took the horses from the young men as they dismounted, looking critically at the rather 'tucked up' condition of the parson's steed. 'Take Mr. Courtenay's horse to a box and feed him till sundown; then put him into the creek paddock. Go round and tell the hands to roll up in the shed at half-past seven to-night. Mr. Courtenay will hold service.' The groom touched his hat with a gesture of assent, and departed with his charge.

The principal sitting-room at Maroobil was a fairly large apartment, which did not aspire to the dignity of a drawing-room. In the days of his father and mother Harold had always remembered them sitting there in the evenings after the evening meal had been cleared away. There was a large old-fashioned fireplace, where in winter such a fire glowed as effectually prevented those in the room from being cold. A solid mahogany table enabled any one to read or write thereon with comfort. And Harold was one of those persons who was unable to pass his evenings in a general way without doing more or less of both. A well-chosen library, with most of the standard authors and a reasonable infusion of modern light literature, filled up one end of the room. Sofas and lounges helped to redeem the room from stiffness or discomfort. Full-length portraits in oil of Harold's father and mother, as also of a preceding generation, with an admiral who had fought at Trafalgar, adorned the walls.

A stag's head and antlers shot in New Zealand, with a brace of stuffed pheasants and the brush of an Australian-bred fox, were fixed over doorways. Guns and rifles of every kind of size, gauge, and construction filled a couple of racks. All things were neat and scrupulously clean, but there was that total absence of ornamentation which characterises a bachelor establishment of a settled and confirmed type.

In the evening, when the master of the establishment and his clerical guest walked across the half-mile which separated the wool-shed from the house— another old-world institution absurdly near the homestead, as the overseer, a 'Riverina man' of advanced views, declared—a fairly numerous congregation was assembled. The chairs and forms had been conveniently placed for the people. The wool table had been dressed up, so as to be made a serviceable reading-desk. Candles in tin sconces lit up the building—a matter which had been found necessary during theatrical representations in the same building during the shearing season, when travelling troupes of various orders of merit essay to levy toll on the cash earnings so freely disbursed at such times.

It was a representative gathering, in some respects a strange and pathetic assemblage. It was known that Mr. Atherstone particularly wished all his employees to attend these occasional services, and to pay due respect to whatever clergyman, in the exercise of his vocation, might find his way to Maroobil. Harold was unprejudiced as to denominations, although firmly attached to his own, and exacted as far as possible a decent recognition of the trouble and personal expenditure undertaken for the spiritual welfare of the neighbourhood.

On the nearest form might be seen the unmistakable type of the English peasant from Essex. The gardener, John Thrum, and his wife, had emigrated from Bishop-Stortford thirty years ago, and finding a congenial resting-place at Maroobil, had remained there ever since, saving their money, and at the beginning of every year expressing their determination to 'go home to England.' A dozen station hands and boundary riders exhibited bronzed and sunburnt features, darkened almost to the complexion of 'Big Billy,' the black fellow, who, with a clean shirt and a countenance of edifying solemnity, sat on one of the back benches. A score of young men and lads, long of limb, rather slouching of manner, with regular features and athletic frames, showed a general resemblance in type, such as that towards which the Anglo-Celtic and Anglo-Saxon Australian is gradually merging. A few women and children, a stray hawker, a policeman on the track of horse-stealers, resplendent in spotless boots and breeches—*voilà tous*! There were Roman Catholics among the crowd, but much abiding in the backwoods had rubbed off prejudice. Padres were scarce, anyhow. There was no chapel within fifty miles, and they didn't think it would be any harm to come.

For the rest, the service of the Church of England, slightly condensed, was gone through; a plain, serviceable sermon, sound in doctrine and not above the heads of the hearers, was administered; the benediction was said; and the little congregation composed of such different elements dispersed—some of them certainly soothed and comforted by the familiar words, if by nought else; others, let us hope, induced to consider or amend their course of life, where such was needful.

As the young men strolled home back to the homestead the clergyman, after a pause, said, 'It often oppresses me with a feeling of sadness, the doubt which I feel whether any appreciable good results from these occasional services, the efforts of myself and other men, who labour under different titles in the Lord's vineyard. When we reflect on the lives these men, almost without exception, lead—the old gardener, perhaps, the sole exception, and the women and children—a man may well doubt whether he is not wearing out his life for nought.'

'It's hard to say,' answered Harold. 'If the soldier does not fight, the battle is not won. One does not see much improvement, certainly, from decade to decade. Perhaps there is less of the open, reckless profligacy that we used to hear of in our boyhood. But no doubt most of the men that we saw to-night gamble, drink, and in riotous living of one form or other dispose of their yearly wages; confessedly going to town at Christmas, or some other holiday, to "knock it down."'

'All of them?' said the preacher. 'Surely there must be some of them who do not?'

'Well, not the married men perhaps—those who have farms and who live in the cooler regions, near the foothills, as the Americans say, of the great mountain-chain. They save their money, and take it home to their wives; it helps for harvest and other time of need. But the older men, the regular nomadic hands, who are rarely married, and the boys, save nothing, except for a grand annual carnival, which after a month leaves them penniless for another year.'

'A practice which must have the most demoralising effect upon these poor victims of drink and debauchery?'

'I really can't say that it has,' replied Harold Atherstone. 'That is the extraordinary part of it. That grizzled, clean-shaved man with the square shoulders and highly respectable English appearance is a Devonshire man, who came here early in life. He has been employed on Maroobil, off and on, ever since I remember. He never drinks when at work. You might send him into the township with a five-pound note any day and he would return sober. He is as hard as nails. I would take his word as soon as any friend I know. He is brave, honest, hard-working, simple. As a labourer he is without a fault. He is the stuff of which England's best soldiers and sailors are made. And yet ____,'

'And yet what?'

'He is a hopeless and irreclaimable drunkard. He has collected his knock-about money, his shearing, and his harvest money about the end of January. By the first or second week in March he has not a shilling in the world—starting out "on the wallaby," as he calls it, sober and penniless, with barely a shirt to his back, trusting to the first job he meets for food and covering. What are you to do with a man like that?'

'Surely a word in season might influence him?'

'Not if one rose from the dead.

'Because, now consider the case carefully, as Mr. Jaggers says. Here is a man who has self-denial enough, with the raging drunkard's thirst upon him, to suddenly determine to abstain wholly, solely, and absolutely from even a teaspoonful of beer, wine, or alcohol, with gallons of it under his nose at every public-house he passes. When you talk to him he is as sober as I am—more so indeed, for I am going to have a glass of whisky and water to-night, whereas he will touch nothing for nearly a year. He says, "Well, master, I be always main sorry at the time, and I do aim not to touch it no more. But the devil, he be too strong for I, and zumhow or zumhow, the old feeling comes over me arter Christmas time, and I knocks all the cheques down, zame as before. But I've neither chick nor child, and I reckon I harm no one but myself."

"'But you'll die in a ditch some day, Ben,' I say to him.

"'Like as not, master," he replies, quite good-humouredly; "and no great matter. A man must die when his turn comes. But you'll have the hay spoiling, master, if you keeps a-talkin' to your hands 'stead of drivin' 'em at their work.'"

'How it must ruin their constitution!' groaned the clergyman. 'They can't have a healthy pulse or movement.'

'Even that is not borne out by fact,' said the squatter. 'Have up this old private in the industrial army, and what do you find? His eye is clear, his cheek is healthy and brown. Let either of us, fairly strong men—taller and broader too—stand alongside of him at a hard day's work, and see where we shall be! Every muscle and sinew, strained and tested since childhood, is like wire compared to cord. The country-bred Englishman is certainly the best working animal in the world, and I cannot conscientiously say that this man's bodily or mental powers have suffered for the life he has led.'

'Is there no hope, then?' said the young preacher despondingly. 'Must the best and bravest of the race be doomed to this hopeless degradation? The preacher's warning is useless, the kindly master's advice, the teaching of experience, the voice of God. What are we to look to in the future?'

'To the spread of education and the development of intelligence. I see no other safeguard. Ben can neither read nor write. Hundreds like him can do so with difficulty—which amounts to nearly the same thing. A certain reaction sets in after continuous labour. What change or recreation have these barren intelligences so complete, so transforming as the madness of intoxication? With culture—national and universal—will come additional means of recreation a hundredfold multiplied. With the refinement inseparable from education will come the distaste for unbridled debauchery, for the coarse and degrading enjoyments of mere sensuality, for a practice which will have become unfashionable with every grade and every class of society.'

'Then you trust in the millennium of universal education—secular or otherwise—not fearing the communistic and atheistic principles which may

80

be involved by mere mental culture unregulated by religious teaching.'

'So long as the race preserves the attributes which have always distinguished it, so long as the passions disturb the reasoning powers, so long as the body preserves its present relation to the spirit, men will drink to heighten pleasure or to dull pain. But in proportion as the mental powers are developed and refined by culture, so will the vice which we call drunkenness diminish, perhaps disappear. With other results of the tillage of that rich and boundless estate, the nation's mind, so long fallow, so negligently worked, I shall not at present concern myself. I have my own opinion.'

'You will not take anything?' said Atherstone, lighting his pipe as the two men sat over the wide fireplace upon their return from the wool-shed. 'Light wine or spirits you will find on the tray; the aerated water is yonder.'

'I think it better for me to practise what I preach in the matter of intoxicating liquors,' said Mr. Courtenay, filling a large tumbler with the aerated water. 'This is very refreshing—though I do not feel called upon to denounce the moderate use of what was doubtless ordained for wise purposes.'

'I can put your horse in the paddock, and let me drive you over to Corindah,' said the host after breakfast next morning. 'He will be all the better for it, and on return you can make across to Yandah just as well from here. I'll send Jack with you across the bush, and he'll put you on to the main Wannonbah road.'

'Thank you very much, Mr. Atherstone; you are always considerate. I began to think Rover was failing a little; yet I had only ridden him forty miles when I met you.'

'Before lunch-time?' said the other, smiling. 'Well, he is a good horse, and carries you well; only, when you come back from Yandah, I'd put the other nag into commission. Leave Rover here till autumn, and he'll be fat and strong to carry you all the winter. And now, if you have any writing to do before lunch, I must leave you in possession. We'll start at half-past three sharp. There's the library, the writing-table, the house generally, to do as you like with till I come back to lunch.'

Punctually at the appointed hour after lunch the pair of fast-trotting, well-bred buggy horses whirled the two young men away on the track to Corindah, a pathway which, already well-beaten, did not appear to be in danger of becoming faint from disuse.

Arriving before sundown, they were received with unmistakable cordiality by the lady of the house, who explained that Pollie had gone out for a ride with her cousin, but would be home by tea-time. This trifling piece of intelligence did not, strange to relate, appear to add to the satisfaction of either guest. Nor even when the missing damsel came riding in, looking deliciously fresh and exhilarated by the healthful exercise, talking in an animated way to Mr. Bertram Devereux, who, attired with great neatness and mounted upon the handsomest horse that Corindah 'had to its name,' looked like an equestrian lounger from Rotten Row, was their equanimity altogether restored. Harold was reserved and imperturbable as usual—even more so. Mr. Courtenay discoursed gloomily about the low state of morality everywhere apparent in the bush. The rather carefully prepared tea entertainment, to which poor Mrs. Devereux had looked forward with a certain pleasurable anticipation, proved flat and uninteresting.

The attendance was comparatively large in the dining-room of the bachelor's quarters, which Mrs. Devereux had caused to be rigorously cleaned out for the occasion. But it was agreed that the sermon of Mr. Courtenay was not so good as usual; that he had 'gone off' in his preaching, and had not been so pleasant-mannered as was his wont. Mrs. Devereux was lost in astonishment at the variation in his performance and demeanour, and concluded by remarking to Pollie privately that clergymen were uncertain in their ways, and that Mr. Courtenay in particular, must have been overworking himself lately, which accounted for his altered form.

Mrs. Devereux was anxious to confide in Harold about Mr. Charteris' unlucky declaration before his departure, and to assure herself of his approval of her conduct. She knew that the young men were as brothers, and that Mr. Charteris would by no means object to such a proceeding. But Harold said rather sternly that he and Mr. Courtenay must drive home that afternoon: he had work to do, etc.; and in spite of an appealing and surprised glance from Miss Pollie, he adhered to his resolution, and after saying farewell formally, was seen no more.

CHAPTER VII

Though there was nothing overt in the manner of Harold Atherstone upon which she could fasten as showing resentment or offence, yet did Miss Devereux acknowledge in her secret heart a coolness in the demeanour of her old friend which troubled her. He was always so kind, so honest, so considerate. 'Tender and true' expressed her thoughts. She could not think of his disapproval without regret, even pain. He had a way of always being in the right, too. On many occasions had they differed in opinion. She recalled how invariably it had been forced upon her cooler, juster self that his opinion had been correct from the beginning. Suppose, she thought to herself, as she leaned out of the window and watched the stars with strange undefined yearnings, that Harold should be right this time! He had said nothing, only showed by his manner, by his countenance, every inflexion of which she knew so well, that he disliked this increasing intimacy with her cousin. Was it increasing? A mere half-friendship, founded on curiosity, admiration of the unknown, upon her own ideal, enveloping him like a costume at a masquerade.

It is possible that this highly important retrospective process might have proceeded to much greater length and depth of research, that curiously constructed organ the female heart being full of all manner of strange corridors, galleries, and shafts, of utterly unknown measure and limit. But circumstances arose—circumstances which altered the aspect of affairs—which turned temporarily the maiden's thoughts into far other channels.

The season being so exceptionally good, the stock and station being nearly 'able to manage themselves,' as Mr. Gateward expressed it, the highly original idea of a summer trip, for the benefit of her own and her daughter's health, suggested itself to the mind of Mrs. Devereux.

'Poor dear! she has been shut up here quite long enough,' said the loving mother. 'I can't say that she doesn't look well, but a voyage must benefit her. It will give a change of ideas. It may take away that restless, discontented feeling which comes to her now so often.'

Thereupon it was decided that they were to go to Sydney, and spend a fortnight among their friends. Then by steamer to Melbourne. From that city they would take one of the New Zealand boats, so as to pass a portion of the summer at the fairy lakes of Rotomahana and the hot springs of Waiwera— that modern imitation of Paradise.

For this unprecedented step Mrs. Devereux had more than one reason. She certainly thought it would tend to her darling's mental and bodily improvement. But that was not all. With womanly quickness sharpened by a mother's instinct, she had divined that the intimacy between Pollie and her cousin was slowly but surely coming closer, nearer, perhaps dearer.

Of the probable *dénouement* she had an instinctive dread. 'I don't know what it is,' she said to herself, 'but I can't altogether put faith in Bertram. It isn't that I can say anything against him. He is clever, manly, good-looking in his way. I didn't think so at first. But somehow I don't seem to be able to know him. He is as great a stranger as the first day I set eyes upon him. Oh! why can't she take Harold Atherstone, who is worth half a dozen of him—of any other man I ever saw, except poor Brian?'

If there was any regret at parting with any one at Corindah, Pollie availed herself of one of the sex's weapons, and reticently made no sign. She appeared to be wild with delight at the

sea-change
Into something rich and strange,

which her daily life was presently to undergo. It may be that she herself was conscious of the slowly increasing power of a fascination which she was powerless to resist. In its present stage—such is the curious, contradictory nature of the maiden's heart—she regarded it with fear and unwillingness.

Thus she caught eagerly at the chance afforded her of a totally new experience, of the strange environments of a delicious foreign existence, such as in the future she might never have the chance of realising under similar conditions. Joyous anticipation seemed to have taken possession of her mind with a sudden rush, forcibly expelling all previous sensations.

Bertram Devereux was chagrined at the change of programme. Coldly self-possessed as usual, however, he betrayed not, by word or manner, his real feeling on the subject.

'Why don't you go home to England while you are about it, Mrs. Devereux?' he asked. 'The time would not be so much longer. You have friends and relations there, and I should be delighted to give you introductions to some of mine.'

'You are indeed most kind,' said the unsuspecting matron, cordially grateful; 'but a voyage to England is too serious a matter to be undertaken lightly. We are doing great things in going to New Zealand and Melbourne. Nothing would induce me to go a step farther, or to stay away more than three or four months at the outside.'

'I feel certain that your daughter would enjoy the European travel. It would be new life to her, and would even benefit you, after your many anxieties,' continued the tempter suavely. 'There'll be nothing to do here or to see to for a couple of years, so Gateward says. You could spare the time well.'

'You seem very anxious to get rid of us,' said the younger lady, with a pout. 'Some people will think six months a long time to miss us from Corindah.'

'Can you think *I* shall not miss you?' returned he, with a sudden change of tone and expression which thrilled her in a manner for which she could not account, as he bent his searching, steadfast gaze upon her. 'But you ought to see the "kingdoms of the world and the glory of them" now that you have the opportunity. I should follow you, mentally, all the way.'

Here one of his rare smiles lit up his face, as he gazed at her with the tenderness one bestows on a child; and again her eyes sank under his, while a faint flush tinged her snow-fair cheek.

'Mother and I cannot make up our minds to such an expedition as going to England all at once,' she replied slowly. 'We require to be educated up to it. Wait until we return from New Zealand, then we will fold our wings, and perhaps make ready for a longer flight.'

'"Would I were, sweet bird, like thee!"' hummed Mr. Devereux, as he gracefully declined further controversy. 'Some of these days you will awake to your privileges, I suppose. We all develop by unmarked changes, none the less surely, however, as fate decrees.'

Mrs. Devereux grew, indeed, half afraid of the momentous enterprise on which she was about to enter. Supported, however, by her daughter, she kept up to the task of packing and providing for departure. This eventually took the form of being driven to the nearest railway terminus, a short day's journey, and being deposited in a first-class carriage, with all their effects in the brake-van, carefully labelled. The next morning saw them in Sydney, the Sea-Queen of the South, somewhat nervously excited at being so far from Corindah, so immeasurably removed from their ordinary life.

'After all,' cried Pollie, as they sat in the balcony of their hotel after breakfast, and gazed over the matchless sea-lake, gay with boats of every size and shape, and the argosies of all lands, while beyond lay the grand eternal mystery of ocean, guarded only by the grim sandstone portals, against which so many ages of tidal force have foamed and raged—'after all we make too much of leaving home for a few months' travel. What wonders and miracles stay-at-home people miss! What human limpets they are; and how narrow are their paths to enjoyment! "I feel as if I were in Paradise, in Paradise,"' she warbled. 'Oh, what a change from our dear old monotonous Corindah!'

'Home is very sweet after all,' said the elder woman, 'though I enjoy this lovely sea-view. But, my darling, you frighten me by these expressions of wild delight. It cannot be good for any one to revel in pleasure, the mere luxurious sensation of change of scene, so intensely, so passionately as you do. Such feelings are unsafe for women. You should moderate them, or evil may come to you from these very unchecked emotions.'

'My darling old mother, I am positively shivering with delight; but why should this or any other natural impulse be wrong? Surely we are given these feelings, like the rest of our nature, for wise reasons? Like speech, laughter, thought, they are unutterable mercies, to be reasonably used and economised. But I see your meaning, and I will guard my emotions a little. I must do so when I get to the hot springs Eden, or I shall be plunging into hot water in mistake for tepid. Fancy a heroine of romance boiled alive!'

'Don't talk of it, my darling,' said Mrs. Devereux, with a shudder. 'Really, don't you think Melbourne will be quite far enough, and very pleasant at this time of year? We might leave New Zealand till another time.'

'Not for worlds,' said the steadfast damsel. 'I want to get a little nearer to the pole. I shall feel like an Arctic explorer.'

The pleasures of the metropolis, doubly sweet after a lengthened absence, had been sipped for a fortnight, when a breezy morn saw the ladies of Corindah steaming out of the harbour on board the *Cathay*, a magnificent sea-monster of the P. and O. persuasion, containing all kinds of delicious foreign novelties, social and material.

'Mother, I don't think I can have been really alive before,' exclaimed Pollie, as they walked down the splendid flush deck. 'I suppose I was living, but I must have been in a state of torpor, with a few mechanical senses feebly revolving, as it were. Isn't this unutterably lovely—quite an eastern fairy-tale in action? Look at those splendidly ugly Seedees in the engine-room, ghouls and afreets every one; besides, even the lascars—what classic profiles and lithe, graceful shapes they have! I feel in love with everybody and everything, down to the Chinese waiters in spotless white.'

When the heads were cleared, and the strong north-easter sent the *Cathay* flying south at the rate of fifteen knots per hour, the motion was increased and perhaps complicated, whereupon an entirely new class of sensations succeeded those of rapturous delight in Pollie's case, in consequence of which a hasty descent into the cabin was rendered necessary.

The morning, however, brought smoother seas and a less urgent breath from Æolus. The naturally strong constitution of the girl triumphed over temporary *malaise*, and soon she was enabled to sit upon deck and enjoy the brilliant and wondrous succession of sea and shore and sky pageants unrolled before her.

A full complement of passengers, bound to and from all parts of the world, had been received on board, so that Pollie's observant eye and sympathetic mind had full employment as the long rows of chairs became gradually filled. People for India, *viâ* Ceylon; home-returning officers and civilians having exhausted their furlough; globe-trotters who had traversed the Australian world from Dan to Beersheba and found all barren, or 'not half a bad place,' according to the state of their living or their reception in clubs and coteries; home-returning Australians, visiting Europe for the first time in their lives, or after many years; mere intercolonial voyagers like themselves; a successful gold-digger or two, treating themselves to first-class passages, plain of aspect, but reserved and correct of manner, as such men generally are, whatever may be said to the contrary by superficial scribes. After Pollie had got over her astonished delight at the *Arabian Nights* portion of the ship, she found a new world of interest and romance opening before her eyes in the Anglo-Saxon section comprising the first-class passengers. This was not lessened in any way when, lunch being announced, she found her mother and herself placed in seats of honour on the right hand of His Majesty the Captain—such being his royal command—while the wife of an eminent Indian civilian looked indignantly and incredulously at them from the opposite side of the table.

It had leaked out through a Sydney friend of Captain Belmont's that this was *the* Mrs. Devereux of Corindah and her daughter, who had taken their passages in the *Cathay en route* to New Zealand, persons of fabulous wealth, girl sole heiress, could not be worth less than a hundred thousand, besides freehold property, and so on. Now Pollie was unquestionably the belle of the ship, and persons of prepossessing appearance were not scarce either; but the slight paleness and languor produced by her unwonted sensations had given her haughty beauty a tinge of softness which, when she issued from her cabin, made her positively irresistible. So the captain, an experienced but susceptible bachelor, had avowed with many nautical asseverations, and thereupon directed the purser, a most distinguished individual in uniform, whom Pollie took to be an admiral at least, to induct them into the place of honour.

When a glass of claret and Selters-water, insisted upon by the captain as a medical necessity, and some slight refection from the luxuriously appointed table had revived the spirits of both ladies, Pollie was enabled to realise her position. Here was she, seated almost upon the dais in point of social elevation, above the wives and daughters of the military, civil, and mercantile swells, palpably receiving the most assiduous attention from the acknowledged autocrat of their *monde*—of that loftiest, most resistless of despots, that uncrowned king, the captain of a crack ocean steamer on board his own ship.

Besides his dazzling and unquestioned superiority, Captain Belmont was a handsome, striking-looking man. Courteous, polished even in manner, he had the eagle eye, the air of resolute command, with which years of unquestioned authority invest the sea-king. Prompt, watchful, fearless, scorning sleep or fatigue when danger menaced, the arbiter of freedom or imprisonment within his own realm, the guardian of every life so confidently entrusted to his care —where is the man who to the maiden's heart, during the long reveries of a sea voyage, so amply fills the character of a hero of romance as the captain? Who has not marked his influence in danger's darkest hour, when the moaning wind, rising fast to the shriek of the tempest, the lurid sky, the labouring bark, and 'the remorseless dash of billows,' all speak to the fear-stricken crowd of dread endings, of wreck in mid-ocean? In such an hour how does every eye turn to the calm, resolute seaman, who directs every act, who foresees the need of every rope that is drawn, of every turn of the helm! How does every listener hang upon his words and dwell upon his lightest syllable of hope!

Has no one seen the grateful company of passengers when land was reached, and, as they deemed, through his skill and vigilance those lives were saved which, in the hour of deadly peril, he held in the hollow of his hand—gather around the captain to express such words of grateful confidence as are seldom yielded to man, the women tearful, the men pressing to shake his hand with honest friendliness? Such a meeting took place, after a dangerous voyage, in honour of one who for twenty years had worthily borne the name of being one of Britain's best and boldest seamen. And the impression on the mind of one eye-witness was never effaced.

It was, therefore, a new and intoxicating position in which Miss Pollie Devereux found herself. The acknowledged object of respectful admiration to this resplendently heroic character, and on equal terms with all the other potentates, from the first officer—a magnificent personage, and second only to the captain in importance—while the rank and file of passengers stood aloof in timid or cynical survey of the damsel whom the Ahasuerus of the hour delighted to honour.

Though partially awed by the eminence of their position, Mrs. Devereux, who had been accustomed in her time to much of respect and consideration, saw nothing very unusual in their promotion. Pollie herself was charmed to find herself on equal conversational terms with such an autocrat. With girlish eagerness she pressed him to tell her of the dangers he had braved and the wonders he had seen. He, nothing loath, produced from time to time, in temptingly small quantities, precious reminiscences of cyclones in the China seas, pirate schooners in the Spanish Main, slavers in Sierra Leone—for he had been in the navy—opium clippers, Chinese mail-boats taken by mutineers and never heard of after, wreck and fire, even all kinds of peril by sea and land in which he had borne a part; so that Pollie or any other damsel might be pardoned for feeling a temporary conviction that such a man had gone through adventures transcending in interest those of the lives of a hundred mere landsmen—that, were the hero of her choice a sailor, she would gladly wear out her life in accompanying him in his voyages.

The next day was Sunday. According to custom, the lascar crew turned out gorgeous in crimson-and-gold scarfs, spotless white robes, and embroidered turbans, very different from their dingy working garb. After breakfast, when the captain in full uniform passed close between the double rank, with the air of Caliph Haroun Al-Raschid, the men lowly salaaming as if thankful not to be doomed to death on that occasion, it was a reproduction in the romantic girl's brain of yet another chapter in the rich traditional glory of the past. Even the Seedees gambolled uncouthly in strange gaudy raiment, looking like slaves who had found an opulent and indulgent master. The while Pollie sat in great state on a cane lounge of honour, with a cushion under her feet and a parasol like the Queen of Sheba's.

Unfortunately for the permanent enjoyment of these dreamy delights, the *Cathay* drove through 'The Rip,' at the entrance to the vast haven at the farther end of which Melbourne commences, on the morning of the third day. A short railway transit saw them deposited at the Esplanade Hotel, where an extended, though not, critically speaking, picturesque sea-view was afforded to them.

Captain Belmont had, with the dash and rapidity which characterise the nautical admirer, obtained Mrs. Devereux' consent to join 'a theatre party' which he had organised. As it happened, an actor of world-wide reputation was performing a favourite melodrama of his own composition. This was a chance, he speciously urged, which Miss Devereux should not be suffered to miss. The promise was made. The captain arrived in due time and escorted them to the Theatre Royal, where one more process of art-magic was added to Pollie's collection.

As their open carriage rolled through the wide, straight streets, in which long rows of lamps glittered on either side, or faded star-like in the far distance, they were impressed with the utterly different expression of Melbourne from that of their own fair city by the sea.

'What a wonderful place!' said Pollie, gazing up the great street which contains all the pleasures and palaces, and is nightly crowded with their votaries. 'How the lamps glow and shimmer! What a vast size and almost sombre uniformity in the buildings which line the streets! There is something weird, too, in the electric lights which create a pale daylight around those endless colonnades. I feel as if I had been transported to some city raised by the wand of an enchanter.'

'Not unlike a little sorcery,' said one of the party, 'when you come to think. There were gum-trees and blacks here "in full blast" half a century ago. Here we are at the Royal.'

It was a command night. The representative of Her Majesty had signified his intention of being present. One of the best boxes in the dress-circle—but two distant from the vice-regal compartment—had been secured by the forecasting captain. The house was crammed. As the popular governor and his party entered, the great assemblage rose like one man to the air of the National Anthem, which aroused Pollie to a burst of loyal enthusiasm.

'It always brings the tears into my eyes,' she said; 'it looks foolish, but I cannot help it. Something in the old tune and the reverence with which our people always greet it stirs my very heart's core. I suppose these feelings are hereditary.'

'The colonies are wonderfully loyal,' said the captain. 'I never saw anything like it. You are more English than the English themselves.'

'I hope we shall always remain so,' said Mrs. Devereux, 'though I believe at home they think we must be essentially different. But the curtain rises. Now, Pollie!'

It follows, as a thing of course, that the whole party, and more particularly Pollie, with her sensitive nature, appreciative as well of the lightest touches of humour as the deeper tones of pathos, were charmed with the play, which had enthralled London nightly for a whole year.

When, after the finale, the party adjourned to the carefully appointed supper which the gallant captain had insisted upon providing—when, amid the popping of champagne corks, a flow of pleasant criticism and enjoyable badinage went round—Pollie realised that she was tasting one of those highly flavoured, almost forbidden pleasures of life which she had read of, but hardly dared to think of sharing.

'This sort of thing is too good to be true,' she replied to Captain Belmont, who was expressing his general and particular satisfaction with 'the way things had gone off.' 'There is so much enjoyment that it must be a little sinful. Don't you think so? I shall wake to-morrow to find it all a dream; or mother will decide that I am never to go to a theatre party again.'

The captain murmured that all manner of delights—the joys that embellish existence—were in her power. She had but to speak the word, doubtless, and slaves in scores would be at her command, himself among the number, only too happy to administer to her slightest wish now and for his whole life after. Here the captain's deep voice faltered, and his expressive eyes, which had done only too much execution in their day, were fixed on hers with an ardent, well-nigh magnetic gaze. The girl trembled involuntarily for a moment, and then laughed lightly, as she replied, 'Is that out of a play, Captain Belmont? I think I have heard it somewhere before. But I feel as if we all belonged to the opera, and that even compliments of that sort chime in with our condition in life.'

The captain's expression changed to one almost gravely paternal as he bowed and trusted she might never meet in after life with friends less sincere than those who would so deeply regret her departure from the *Cathay*. Then, as Mrs. Devereux made the slightly perceptible movement which defined the limit of the symposium, they joined the retreat, and the captain surrendered whatever illusion he may have cherished concerning his too charming passenger.

CHAPTER VIII

After the splendour and distinction of the *Cathay*, the voyage to New Zealand was a tame affair, voted so even by Mrs. Devereux. Both ladies were heartily glad when the wooded heights of the Britain of the South rose from the underworld, and they addressed themselves to the great question of disembarkation with earnestness.

Of their stay in the land of the Maori and of their enjoyment of the daily supply of delights and wonders, it were superfluous to tell; of Pollie's reverential admiration for the first Rangatira whom she encountered—a grizzled, war-worn chief who had fought stubbornly against us at the Gate Pah, and had in his day killed (and eaten) many a tribal foe. Upon the brilliant verdure of the pasture refreshed by the perennial moisture of a sea-girdled isle, the hawthorn hedges, the roadside ditches, the old-world English look of so many things and people, she was never tired of expatiating. The people, the scenery, the climate, and the soil were new. The forests of strange glossy-leaved trees, of noble pines, of clinging parasites with crimson blossoms, held neither bird, nor beast, nor leaf, nor flower akin to those of the Australian continent.

'What a wonderful region! So near to us—a few days' voyage only—and yet so unlike. And what a sheep country! No dingoes, no eagles, no snakes, no crows! This last is simply incredible. Fancy a country without crows! There must be something wrong about it. What would Mr. Gateward say? And such grass! If we only could have "travelled" over here in the drought! It seems hard that Providence devoted all the intervening distance to water. Had it been dry land, it would have been worth all the rest of our continent.'

'"The earth is the Lord's and the fulness thereof," my darling,' said the mother. 'I don't like to hear you talk lightly about such things. Seas and lands were doubtless arranged as they are for some wise purpose.'

'I never meant to be irreverent, my dearest. I was only thinking what a pity this fine south latitude region should be useless. Only fancy, except this little New Zealand dot, there is no habitable land between us and the South Pole. Oh! I forgot the Crozets—those islands where the ship was wrecked, and the passengers were cast away nearly twelve months. All their hair turned white as fleeces. So complexion is only a matter of latitude after all.'

Their time was all too short when the route was again given, and the party with which they had amalgamated proceeded by tourist stages to the dream-region of Rotomahana.

92

Of the glories and triumphs of that wonderland who shall tell adequately, who depict with a tithe of the fresh brilliant colouring that Nature—earliest of Royal Academicians—has invented?

'I will never go back,' quoth Pollie; 'here I will live and die. I will become a guide, like Maori Kate here—magnificent creature that she is! I will never be proud of civilisation again. What do we get by it forsooth? Headaches, neuralgia, nervous systems, toothaches, and shortened lives. These noble Maoris never have headaches, except from too much rum—which is only a transient, not a chronic ailment—but unfailing appetite, health, strength and activity; hair that doesn't come out or turn bald and grey; teeth that serve to reduce food and not to enrich dentists. I say we are manifestly inferior to this noble people. Why do we want to conquer them or convert them?'

'My darling,' said Mrs. Devereux, 'this air is too stimulating; I am afraid you are going out of your mind. It will never do for you to go on in England like this. Fancy what your father's family would think!'

'I shall sober down before we take our European tour,' answered the young lady. 'I shall have something to talk about, though, shan't I? And we must go through Paris; I don't want to be "bonneted" metaphorically (that's rather neat, dear, between ourselves) because my headgear is not up to the fashionable cousins' standard. But I think I could hold my own. I shall begin by being *very* simple, and having things explained to me that I have known all my life; then dawn on them by degrees.'

'My darling, you only need to be your own dear, sweet self, and be assured you will be able to hold your own with any people you are likely to meet at home or abroad. I don't wish my pet to affect anything, either below or above her. You have great natural gifts, a fairly good education, and what experience you are deficient in will always be made up by your unusual quickness of comprehension. That is your old mother's honest opinion, and she would not deceive you for the world.'

'And I care not two straws for anybody else in comparison, you dear old darling. You are ever so clever too—if you were not so unreasonably diffident about yourself. However, I will educate you when we reach England. You'll see the firm of "Pollie and Mother" will achieve distinction.'

The summer joys passed all too quickly. Why cannot one remain in fairyland? Perhaps as the years rolled on we should hear one morning a dismal summons. The faces of our gay companions would undergo a terrible alteration. The dread messenger had arrived who was to exact 'the teind for hell.' Thus it ran in the old ballad. So True Thomas found it. The fairy flowers withered, the fay faces changed. All was pale, awesome. The day of payment for pleasure unstinted and unhallowed joys had arrived.

There is always a day of reckoning, a reactionary change from pleasant sojourns. True Thomas lies beneath the 'knowe' at Ercildoune. Our modern fairies are clad in tulle and tarlatan; are seen beneath electric lights. Old faiths are crumbling. They lie—like 'ancient thrones'—in the workrooms of scientists and positivists. Yet still is there a flavour of the old-world belief which clings about us. Remorse and regret, passion and despair, survive. And even as we return from the land of pleasure along paths of duty, the refrain sounds sadly in our ears that all earth's joys are fleeting; that the ocean of eternity must be the end of life's bark; that its tideless waves may ever be heard, deeply dirgeful, in the intervals of vanity and madness.

So, when the first Australian winter month—that of May—found the travellers again *en route* for Corindah, where everything bade fair to be as quiet and peaceful as on the day they left, Pollie's first feeling was one of indefinable regret. 'I could almost wish we had never left home, mother,' she said; 'everything will look so quiet and dull till we regain our eyesight. It looks mean and ungrateful to the dear old place and our friends to go back to them as a kind of *pis aller* after having exhausted the pleasures of vagabondising. I suppose we shall drop into our old sleepy ways again by degrees. We are such creatures of habit.'

'For my part, I am thankful to get back,' said Mrs. Devereux. 'My dear garden will be looking so well, as I see that they have had rain. I quite pine for a little needlework, too. I miss my steady pursuits, I must say.'

'Garden!' said Pollie disdainfully; 'a pretty garden it will look after the bright rata and laurel thickets, the ancient groves of totara and kauri, the ferny dells of Waitaki! It seems like growing mustard and cress upon a yard of damp flannel, as I used to do in my childhood. However, as I said before, our tastes will recover themselves I hope.'

———————————

Corindah once more. Again the endless grey-green plains—the sandhills—the myall—the mogil—the familiar, not ungraceful, but sparse and monotonous woodland—the wire fences stretching for scores of miles on every side—the gates all of the same pattern—the hundreds of thousands of merino sheep, each unit undistinguishable from another save by the eye of experience—the blue heaven—the mirage—the boundary riders—the men—the horses—the collie dogs—all moving in unvarying grooves, as if they had never done anything else since the travellers departed, and were incapable of change, emotion, or alteration.

However, as the buggy from the station drove through the well-remembered gate, Harold Atherstone, with Bertram and Mr. Gateward, were there to meet the home-returning travellers. The evident pleasure in each face touched the girl's heart, and she pressed the gnarled hand of the overseer with considerably more cordiality than she was in the habit of putting into her greetings, as she replied to the general expression of welcome.

'Thought you'd followed my advice and taken the New Zealand mail-steamer for England,' said Mr. Devereux, with his usual calmness of intonation, though a flush on his ordinarily pale cheek betrayed suppressed emotion. 'I should have done so in your case I know.'

'I daresay they have only come home to pack now,' said Harold. 'A taste for travel, once acquired, is never shaken off—by women at any rate. The West Logan must look like the Soudan after your late experiences.'

'You are all very unkind,' said Pollie; 'that is, except Mr. Gateward, who is too glad to see us to make rude speeches. Don't we enjoy coming home like other people with hearts? We are not going away for years, are we, mother?'

'Not if my wishes are consulted, my dearest,' said Mrs. Devereux, stretching her neck to look over the garden paling. 'I want rest, and time to think my own thoughts and enjoy a little quiet life again.'

'You have come to the right "shop" for that, as I heard one of the boundary riders say to-day, my dear Mrs. Devereux,' said Bertram. 'Anything more uniform, not to say monotonous, than our lives here in your absence cannot be imagined. Nothing ever happens here, now that the excitement of the drought is over.'

'I heard some news by telegram before I came over,' said Harold, 'which is likely to cause a stir in the district. It's rather bad of its sort, and may lead to worse results even.'

'Thank God for it, anyhow!' said Bertram; 'anything is better than the dead level of dulness we have lately been reduced to. What is it?'

The other man looked grave. 'It's not a matter to be lightly treated. Two bushrangers are "out." They shot dead one of the escort troopers from Denman Gaol to Berrima, overpowered the others, and are now at large at no great distance from Wannonbah.'

'Oh!' said Mrs. Devereux, turning pale, 'I am so sorry. Not that I feel frightened; but now that they have shed blood, and must suffer if taken, they are desperate men, and will scarcely be taken alive. Do you know their names?'

'The younger man is Billy Mossthorne; as for the other, I don't know. He is an old offender. The police are, of course, all over the district. Sergeant Herne passed Maroobil in an old slouched hat and plain clothes, but one of the men knew him and told me. He will run them down if any one can. Every trooper in the North-West is out.'

'But what chance in a country like this will he have?' said Bertram. 'The outlaws are miles away by this time, and can easily cross the border into Queensland. I'd take short odds they are never seen again.'

Mr. Atherstone smiled. 'He has the chance of the sleuth-hound on the trail of the deer. The police force of this colony is well organised. Mossthorne is a horseman, a bushman, and a dare-devil not easily matched; but there are as good men as he on his track.'

'If the brutes would only come into the open,' said Bertram, with his quiet sneer, 'one would be saved the bother of thinking about them. They haven't pluck enough for that, I expect.'

'To do them justice,' replied Atherstone, 'they don't lack the old English virtue of bulldog courage, as any one will find that meets them under fire. Personally, I should not be grieved if they got away to the "Never Never country," and were not heard of again. Mossthorne worked for me once. He was a fine manly young fellow, and I have always regretted deeply that he got into bad company and worse ways. In the front of a line regiment or on a quarter-deck, Billy would have shown what stuff he was made of, and his country might have been proud of him.'

'I have no sympathy with such ruffians, old or young,' said Devereux. 'The sooner they are hanged or shot the better, and I should like to have the chance of putting a bullet into either of them.'

'I daresay I shall shoot as straight as any one else if it comes to a scrimmage,' said the other; 'but I can't help mourning over a good man spoiled. That they will not be taken alive, we may make tolerably sure.'

At the commencement of the conversation Mrs. Devereux had turned pale. The sad memories of the past were awakened. She took the first opportunity of retiring with her daughter, leaving the young men to their argument.

'And what have you done with yourself all the time?' said Pollie to her cousin, as they sat at breakfast next morning. 'It does seem so hard to have been shut up here while we were in Fairy-land—were we not, mother?' she said, appealing to Mrs. Devereux, who sat in her place with rather an abstracted air.

'What were you saying, my dear? Oh! yes, delightful, was it not? I was just thinking that we need not have hurried back. Did you go anywhere, Bertram, or see any society in our absence?'

'I went to Bourke for a fortnight?' he answered, with a smile in which there was more sarcasm than merriment. 'I was afraid to trust myself within the fascination of real civilisation, so I declined Melbourne or Sydney.'

'And what did you think of that desert city?' inquired Pollie, with mock humility. 'Did Your Royal Highness find anybody fit to talk to?'

'It struck me as a queer place,' he said. 'You could not expect me to have seen anything like it before. But it wasn't bad in its way. The weather was glorious. The men were better than I expected. Rather fast, perhaps. Their manners lacked repose. They took care no one else should have any, as they kept it up all night most of the time I was there. One young fellow jumped his horse over the hotel bar—a thing I had previously taken to be pure fiction, on the American pattern.'

'That's rather old-fashioned bush pleasantry,' said Pollie; 'he must have been very young. How did the horse like it?'

'I don't know, but he did it cleverly. I expected to see both their necks broken and the smash general; but all came right by a miracle, and the fellow won his bet—twenty pounds. I heard him make it.'

'And was that the only style of society you encountered?' queried Pollie, with a disdainful and disapproving air. 'You could have enjoyed that at Wannonbah.'

'Permit me. I did not enjoy it; I only observed it. But there were really some nice fellows, who had just come over from Queensland—Lord Harrowsby's younger brother, and Thoresby, a Suffolk man, whose cousin I was quartered with once. They had just been investing in a sugar plantation, and were going to make a fortune in three years. One of the local men asked us all out to his place. Drove four-in-hand, too. We had a famous week of it. I never expected to enjoy it so much. Lived in a really good style.'

'Wonderful, when you come to think of it,' said the girl saucily, 'that any one should have a decent establishment in Australia! But you'll make discoveries by degrees.'

'I'm afraid you're laughing at me,' he said gravely. 'I am not of a sanguine disposition, I own. I didn't expect *anything* when I came here. But perhaps I shall have fewer mistakes to retract than if I had been imaginative.'

'I am not laughing at you; indeed, I think you wonderfully wise and prudent for the time you have been out. By and by you will know everything that we do ourselves. But what always entertains me about you recent importations is the mild air of surprise with which you regard the smallest evidence that the men that preceded you, and built up these great cities, this wonderful country, were of much the same birth, breeding, and social status as ourselves.'

'But many were not, surely? That must be admitted.'

'The majority were; the leaders, certainly, in every branch of civilisation: how else would the miraculous progress have been effected? The rank and file were much like other people—good, bad, and indifferent.'

Once more the old life was resumed at Corindah. Once more the succession of easy tasks and simple pleasures obtained. The walks by the river-side—the rides and drives—the history readings—the French and Italian lessons—the peaceful mornings when tranquil Nature seemed assured against change, disturbance, or decay—the dreamy afternoons—the long, quiet evenings divided between books, music, and an occasional game of whist for Mrs. Devereux's entertainment when Harold Atherstone came over. As the weeks glided on, Pollie could not believe that she had ever left Corindah, that the voyages, the travel, the strange people and incidents were unrealities, fashioned of 'such stuff as dreams are made on.'

She had resumed her quasi-friendly relations with Bertram Devereux, who apparently had not noticed the alteration of her feelings towards him. With his accustomed patience he had accepted the position, and merely set himself to overcome her doubts and maidenly scruples. In this attempt his knowledge of the subject assured him that he would ultimately succeed.

Harold Atherstone certainly came pretty frequently. He was not a man to be lightly regarded as a rival. 'What a stir he would have made in some places that I have known!' thought Devereux to himself. 'That *grand seigneur* air of his, the height, the stalwart frame, his Indian-chief sort of immobility, joined to his consummate skill in all accomplishments of an athletic nature. Here,' he said to himself, with a sardonic smile, 'he is thrown away. The type is more common than with us, and he has the fatal drawback, in the eyes of our *prima donna*, of too early, too familiar, too brotherly an intimacy. She knows him like a book. With the perverse instinct of her sex, she despises the well-read, dog's-eared volume, full of high thought and purpose, and longs for a newer work—inferior, possibly, as it may be, but with uncut pages. I shall win this game, I foresee, as I win the odd trick at our little whist tournaments—by superior science, even against better cards. Well, what then? As the husband of the handsomest woman of her year, with Corindah for her ultimate dowry, and a handsome allowance, I suppose one could live in London. Ah! would it not be life again? Not this vegetable existence, which one can stand for a year or two, but dull, dismal, *à faire peur*, after a while.'

Had the intensity of the feeling which Bertram Devereux had reached reacted upon the girl's sensitive organisation? No alteration of manner, or one so trifling that it could hardly be perceived, had taken place. Still, like the swimmer on the smoothly gliding tide which leads to the whirlpool or the rapids, she felt conscious of a hidden force, which became daily more difficult to analyse or resist.

Had any one told her, upon the arrival of Bertram Devereux at Corindah, that her heart would eventually be forced to surrender at his summons, the proud beauty would have laughed the prophecy to scorn. But now, when with pensive brow and thoughtful air she searched its recesses, and examined the feelings which held possession of her waking thoughts, she could not deny that the image of the stranger had no rival to fear, no refusal to dread, in the fateful hour which would decide two destinies.

But in the intervals of distrust which disturbed her mind—and there were many—one question invariably asserted prominence, one dark spirit of doubt refused to be laid. She knew that Bertram Devereux had lived much in society in early life; had been of the *haute volée* of the great world both in England and abroad. Was it possible that he should have been a recognised figure in those luxurious, exclusive circles without having given his heart to some one of the fascinating personages which there abounded?

Were it so, would it be possible that he had pledged himself, unalterably, irrevocably, to return from Australia and fulfil his promise within a certain time? Englishmen often did this, and when time had altered their ideas, or loosened the bonds which in good faith should have remained inflexible, married some girl that took their fancy in the colonies, and quietly settled down for life in the land of their adoption. But such a lover should not be hers, she told herself. He who for gold or light love forfeited his pledged word was a forsworn coward. She could not for an instant brook the idea of being mentally compared with the former occupant of a heart every pulse of which should beat for her and her alone. She knew that every thought, every aspiration, every fibre of her being would be blended in the existence of her lover. Proud, sensitive, unconsciously exacting, even jealous, the fierce blood she inherited from Brian Devereux boiled up as she thought of the indignity, the degradation of sharing in such a sense the affections of any living man. She did not rise from her long musing fit on that still, dreamy, silent eve without telling herself, that in the probable case of Bertram Devereux declaring himself, he should satisfy her fully upon this point, or hand of hers should never clasp his before the altar.

While the great hope which arises in every human breast was perfecting itself —that flower which blooms so fair, or pales and fades untimely, was daily ripening, tending towards fragrance and fruition—the little world of West Logan was apparently stationary. The vast green prairies were commencing to grow yellow before the warm breezes of the early summer; the days were lengthening; the dark-blue gold-fretted nights were shorter; the dawn followed midnight with lesser interval. All things appeared calm and changeless as a summer sea. The stormy ways of evil deeds, crime, and death seemed as improbable as messages from another planet.

Strangers came and went, but they were principally camp-followers of the great armies of sheep which from time to time, being mobilised for various reasons, marched from one end of the territory to the other, or to the borders of other colonies. But one evening a shabbily-dressed man, on a rough-looking horse, rode into the stable-yard, where he encountered Mr. Gateward, whom he engaged in serious conversation.

'Who in the world can that be?' asked Bertram irritably, from his seat in the verandah. A book of Rossetti's poems was before him. He had been reading aloud to his cousin. Her work lay unheeded on the Pembroke table. 'Another of those confounded sheep "reporters"! I wish they would stay at home for a time. I am sure Gateward and I are sick of the very sight of travelling sheep.'

'Wait till I take a peep at him,' said the girl. 'He does not look altogether like a sheep man.'

Pollie walked to the end of the verandah, and peeping over the lemon hedge which bounded the garden, examined the stranger with a searching and practised eye.

'His bit and stirrups are rusty. He has an old slouched felt hat, and only one spur. He stoops as he sits in his saddle. Mr. Gateward is looking very serious. What do you make of all that?' she said archly, as she came back to her companion.

'Working overseer—thirty or forty thousand sheep—to be at our boundary gate to-night. Wants to go the inner track, where Gateward is saving the grass. No wonder he looks serious.'

'It would not be a bad guess if matters ran in their ordinary groove; but I see signs of a change, with danger signals ahead. That quiet-looking man is Miles Herne, one of the smartest sergeants in the police force. He has been on the track of the two bushrangers. I saw him two or three years ago, and I don't forget people that interest me. He is here to get information, or to give some that may be important.'

'That man a sergeant of police!' exclaimed Bertram, surprised out of his usual equanimity. 'You must surely be mistaken, or he is a consummate artist in disguise.'

'It is the man himself,' persisted she. 'We Australians have sharp eyes— savage attributes, you know. He has captured many a cattle-stealer, they say, in that unassuming bush attire. There is a good deal of talent among our New South Wales troopers. There was Senior-Constable Ross, who used to be told off to catch sly grog-sellers. His get-up was wonderful. Once, Harold told me, he went as one of a pair of blackfellows, and quite outdid the real aboriginal, securing a conviction too. Go down and see the sergeant. I am uneasy about his errand.'

CHAPTER IX

Before the young man made his way into the stable-yard, Pollie meanwhile retreating to her mother's room, the strange horseman had hung up his steed to a post and followed Mr. Gateward to the barracks, in the sitting-room of which unpretending but useful adjunct to the mansion proper Mr. Devereux found them in earnest conclave. They stopped speaking when he entered. The stranger looked searchingly at the young Englishman, who decided, after encountering the keen grey eye and marking the resolute face and wiry, athletic frame, that no ordinary man was before him.

Gateward, after looking round carefully, began in a tone of solemnity and mysterious import. 'Mr. Devereux, this is Sergeant Herne, stationed at Warban, but now on duty out of uniform, for reasons as you'll understand. He's on the track of the men we've heard on.' The stranger saluted in military style, and Bertram instinctively returned the courtesy in like form. 'And bad news he've heard, I'm afraid,' continued Mr. Gateward.

'The sergeant will tell us himself,' interposed Bertram. 'These bushrangers are in the neighbourhood? We heard that before.'

'It's a trifle worse than that, sir,' said the disguised man-at-arms, unbuckling a leather belt and placing a navy revolver, previously concealed by his coat, upon the table. 'Unless my information is false—and I have every reason to think otherwise—the pair of them, the Doctor and Billy Mossthorne, will be here to-night.'

'Here! good God!' said Bertram. 'Why the deuce should they come here? Fancy having to fight the scoundrels with ladies in the house! Can't we meet them and have it out on the road?'

'It's impossible to say which way they'll come in,' said the sergeant thoughtfully. 'Fellows like them don't travel on roads. They know every inch of the bush from here to the Lachlan, and can go as straight as a blackfellow by night as well as by day. They're hid in the Warrambong scrubs now, it's a good way off, and my men have run them close. But by hard riding they'll get here by midnight, expecting every one in the place to be sound asleep.'

'But what do they want here?'

'It's hard to know what the Doctor wants. He's one of the biggest scoundrels unhanged. But what Bill Mossthorne is after is a couple of your best horses, and as much clothes and grub as'll see them across the Queensland border. He was hurt in the scuffle, and walking in his leg-irons for forty-eight hours gave him a terrible shaking. The Doctor had to carry him on his back part of the last day, I was told.'

'Then we shan't see them until they turn up here?'

'Not if I'm laid on properly,' said the hunter of men. 'Between twelve and one o'clock to-night, if we've luck, they'll drop into as pretty a trap as ever they were in in their lives.'

'The Doctor, as they call that scoundrel—haven't I heard something about him before?' said Bertram musingly. 'It must have been long ago, but I seem to have an indistinct memory concerning him.'

The two others looked meaningly at each other. Then Mr. Gateward spoke.

'Perhaps it will be as well to keep it from the missis, sir. It might shake her a deal, thinkin' on it. But the Doctor's the man that shot her husband thirteen years ago this very month. The Captain hit him hard the same time, and he's been heard to say he'll leave his mark on Corindah yet.'

Bertram Devereux set his teeth, and a smile, such as men wear in the moment of hard and bitter resolve, passed slowly over his face, while his eyes lightened and gleamed, as if he saw his dearest hope realised.

'By God! you don't tell me so?' he said, in so changed a voice that both of the men shifted position and gazed upon him as he spoke. 'What an astonishing coincidence! I wouldn't have missed this night for a fortune. To think, too, that I was so nearly off to that back station this morning, Gateward, wasn't I? And now, sergeant, you are our commanding officer. You have the *carte du pays*. What is the order of the day, or rather of the night?'

The sergeant sat himself composedly down on the substantial table which took up the centre of the apartment, and in a businesslike tone of calculation and arrangement unfolded his plan of action.

'You see, I had only one trooper with me,' he said. 'The rest are round Warrambong Mountains. I sent him with a note to Maroobil. Mr. Atherstone will be here to-night. That will be plenty. We don't want a mob round the place. Some one might show out too soon, and then they wouldn't come. If they're let alone, and come in as I say, we'll get them "to rights." There'll be some close shooting, but they can't get away if we've a rag of luck.'

'Which way will they attempt to enter?' said Bertram, lighting a cigarette. 'Here or at the house?'

'From what I was told,' said the sergeant, with an air of satisfaction, 'they will come to the barracks, to this very room, and a better line—for us—they couldn't have taken. They know this place and all the ins and outs of the premises well. Their dart is to knock up the storekeeper, Mr. Newman, and make him hand over whatever they want—or will—or the cash-box. They know the back entrance from here to the house.'

'Which they'll never set foot in,' said Bertram. 'If we don't give a good account of them here, prepared as we shall be when they turn up, we deserve never to pull trigger again.'

'I've had a few close brushes with men of their sort,' said Herne, with a grim smile of satisfaction, 'but I don't know that ever I saw a neater thing than what we're working now. We've got 'em on toast. You see, sir, what a beautiful room this is?'

Devereux looked round the unadorned apartment with a slight expression of inquiry.

'I mean to be "stuck up in" of course. Don't know that I ever saw the equal of it. They begin in the verandah. We're safe to hear their step or voices. It's all dark, of course. They light a match to rouse up Mr. Newman. They know that's his room on the right-hand side there. You and I stand just inside this bedroom, Constable Gray and Mr. Atherstone about there. The moment they light their match, we call on them to surrender in the Queen's name. Mr. Gateward, who's behind the bale of sheepskins, lights a lantern that stands all ready, so as we can see what we're about, and in a brace of shakes the thing's over.'

'It's quite certain there's no more than two of them, sergeant?' said Mr. Gateward. 'You're sure of that, I reckon. Not that we mind much, but it might make a difference.'

'There might be a third man. I heard that "Johnny the Pacer" was seen at Warrambong the other day. But he's more in the horse-duffing line than where there's shooting going on.'

'However, you never know when these fellows will turn out. There's been a warrant out for him these two years.'

'We shall be all the better matched,' said Bertram. 'The more the merrier, as long as we're only man to man. I wonder Atherstone isn't over yet. I suppose the ladies had better not know anything about the visitors we expect.'

'Begging your pardon, sir,' said Gateward, with a look of resolve upon his face. 'It will be best to put them on their guard. It would give them a shock if they woke up and heard the shooting. They're neither of them ladies as will scream and faint or act with any foolishness.'

'I think Gateward is right,' said the sergeant gravely. 'If they're prepared, depend upon it they'll be brave and steady; ladies mostly are in the real push of danger. And Mrs. Devereux hasn't lived here all these years without knowing about bushrangers, more's the pity.'

'Had reason to know 'em too well,' said the overseer, shaking his head. 'You won't frighten Miss Pollie, sir, and the missus, for, as quiet as she looks, she isn't to say timorsome.'

'I hear horses now,' said the young man. 'Atherstone and your trooper, I suppose. If you think it's best for the ladies to know, we will tell them.'

'And I'll go with Gateward and get something to eat,' said the sergeant. 'I've had a long ride, and nothing's passed my lips since sunrise. We shall all want something before the night's over.'

Harold Atherstone rode into the stable-yard, followed by a slight, wiry-looking young fellow in the uniform of the mounted police. He was mounted upon an upstanding, well-bred bay, and led a saddled roan, the points and condition of which denoted blood, good keep, and regular stabling.

'You'll find spare stalls or boxes there, constable,' said Bertram. 'Charley, the groom, is somewhere about. He'll give you a hand to bed down your horses.'

'This is a queer business, Atherstone,' said he, when the trooper had departed with the horses. 'We shall have sharp shooting if these fellows turn up, and I suppose there's no doubt about it.'

'It will be the first time I ever knew Miles Herne wrong,' said Atherstone, 'if they're not here at the hour he says. I wish to Heaven they had picked Maroobil for their next bit of devilry. However, it can't be helped. It's lucky we were both in the way, and doubly fortunate that we've had timely warning.'

'By Jove! yes,' said the other, 'and I was near as could be going away back this morning. How savage I should have been! Come into my room and dress. I can tell you all about Herne's arrangements. What a smart fellow he is, and as cool as a cucumber!'

'If you'd known all the close things I've seen him in, and the arrests he's made, you'd say so,' replied the other. 'He's the show trooper of the North-West. They always detail him when there's anything specially dangerous to be done. He'll be promoted this time if he bags these fellows, and I hope to Heaven he may.'

When the two young men made their appearance in the dining-room, there was but little need for them to speak.

'I know there is something dreadful the matter,' said Pollie, 'by Harold's grave face. I suspected Sergeant Herne didn't turn up here for nothing. That was a trooper and two police horses that came with you, Harold, was it not? Better tell us at once. Mother is growing pale with anxiety.'

'Do not be afraid for us,' said the widow, with a sad smile. 'I have borne too much sorrow to have room for fear.'

'The whole mighty matter,' said Harold, thinking that he could best describe the affair in the familiar terms which would perhaps divest the intelligence of sudden terror, 'is that Herne has got news of these bushranger fellows. Thinks they might possibly pay Corindah a visit to-night.'

'Is that all?' exclaimed Pollie, her head raised, her face aglow with excitement, while her large bright eyes sparkled with an expression much more akin to pleasurable expectation than fear. 'Why, I thought some one was dead—that some terrible, irrevocable accident had happened. And what time will they arrive? I suppose they won't send in their cards?'

'My darling, do not talk so lightly,' said her mother, whose set, grave expression showed in how different a light she regarded the news. 'These men have blood upon their hands. More will be shed yet, I fear, and whose it may be we know not.'

'We must not be too serious over it either, Mrs. Devereux,' said Atherstone. 'With the preparations we have been able to make and a superior force well armed, the only fear in Herne's mind, I suspect, is that one of their telegraphs may get wind of our plan, and warn them away. About midnight is the time they were likely to be about, if his scouts spoke truly.'

'Why, it will be something like the midnight attack in *Wild Sports of the West*,' said Pollie, 'that I used to devour when I was a tiny girl. Don't you remember, Harold, when the daughter of the house comes in with an apron full of cartridges? Oh! I shall be so disappointed if they don't come after all.'

The young men felt much inclined to laugh at the genuine desire for fight, the keen enjoyment of a probable *mêlée*, which Pollie had evidently inherited with her Milesian blood. But one look at the white face and drawn lips of Mrs. Devereux checked them. 'The names,' she said, 'have you heard the names?'

'One of them is called——' said Bertram, anxious to exhibit his knowledge of the affair.

'Called Mossthorne—William Mossthorne,' interposed Harold, with a meaning look at Devereux. 'The other is a stranger. They are not sure whether he is the man they fancy or not. We shall know if he comes one way or the other.'

Mrs. Devereux looked relieved. Her face had a far-off, dreamy expression, as if she were recalling the old days of sudden misery, of woe unutterable, of hopeless agony, from which she had been so long recovering. But for the bright-eyed girl, that now with eager face and fearless brow brought back her father's very face to her, she told herself that she never would have cared to live. And now, after all these years, the old accursed work was to recommence, with, perhaps, loss of valuable life, with enmity and bloodshed certainly. At their very gates too; beneath their hitherto inviolate roof-tree. When was it all to end?

However, she felt it incumbent on her as the chatelaine to put a brave face upon the matter. There was not the slightest chance of victory on the part of the outlaws, outnumbered and outmatched as they would be. She therefore exerted herself during the remainder of the meal to appear resolute and steadfast. She even gave advice which her long experience of colonial manners and customs enabled her to offer.

'Bertram, above all things, you mustn't be rash,' she said. 'Remember that these are not men to hold cheaply. They are cunning and artful, besides being brave with the desperation of despair. Don't think because you have been a soldier, that these bush brigands are to be despised. My poor husband paid dearly for that mistake.'

The young man looked up cheerfully. 'My dear aunt,' he said, 'I don't despise our friends the bush robbers, or whatever they call them. I think them very ugly customers. Some of the shearers we had the row with last year would be truly formidable with arms in their hands. But I am a consistent fatalist in these matters. One man gets shot in such an affray; around another the bullets rain harmless. If I am fated to drop, I shall do so, and not otherwise.'

'And what are *we* to do all the time?' inquired Pollie, with an air of disapproval. 'Go to bed and sleep? Just as if any one could, with a battle coming off next door. I suppose we must stay quiet till it is all over? What a dreadful thing it is to be a woman!'

'Very likely there won't be any engagement at all; it may not come off,' said Harold. 'So I would not advise you to lie awake on the chance of it. You may lose your rest for nothing. In fact, the chances are six to four—firstly, that they'll surrender directly they see us prepared to receive them; secondly, that they won't come into the barracks at all. They may turn back, like dingoes suspecting a trap.'

'Pray Heaven it may be so!' said Mrs. Devereux. 'I am not unwilling to take my share of the risk and loss for the country's good. But oh! if it should turn out to be a false alarm, how thankful I should be!'

The evening passed off without much to distinguish it from other evenings, momentous as was the contingent finale. Mrs. Devereux was absent and preoccupied. Pollie was alternately in high spirits or depressed and silent. Atherstone and Bertram talked in a matter-of-fact sort of way about things in general, but made no further allusion to the subject which engrossed their thoughts.

At ten o'clock the ladies retired, rather to the relief of the young men. Mrs. Devereux did not omit, however, to again urge upon Bertram the necessity of caution and prudence.

'I shall not risk my precious person unwisely,' he said, a little impatiently; 'but why do you not warn Atherstone here in the same maternal manner? I know you regard him as an old and valued friend. Is he so much more experienced than I—who have done a little soldiering, you will recollect—or is my life more precious than his in your eyes?'

'Harold knows very well,' said the widow simply, 'how I feel towards him. But he can take care of himself among these people, whereas you, my dear Bertram, are at a disadvantage. I do you no injustice when I compare you with my darling husband, who lost his life, as you may do to-night, from contempt of his adversary and want of proper caution.'

'Harold, you are to take care of yourself, and Bertram too. Do you hear?' called out Pollie, who was in the passage. 'You are to tell him what to do, for of course, being newly arrived, he will know nothing. You mustn't be angry, Bertram. All you Jackaroos (as the Queenslanders call you) are the same; you leave cover and get shot down like an owl in the daylight, for want of the commonest woodcraft. So don't be obstinate, or I shall be obliged to come down and stand alongside of you. Good-night! Good-night! That is one apiece.'

When the young men entered the room at the barracks, they found the sergeant and Mr. Gateward sitting over the fire smoking. The young constable was on guard outside, in case the attack might come off earlier than was anticipated.

The sergeant, though in an attitude of luxurious contentment, was in full uniform, and fully prepared for sudden action. By his side stood a Winchester rifle in excellent order, while within reach of his arm was a large-sized navy revolver. Mr. Gateward had girded on one of the same pattern.

'You're all ready, gentlemen, I suppose?' said the officer. 'Both with revolvers, I see. They're pretty tools, but I prefer my rifle for close range. In an hour more we must put out the lights; so you'd better light up, and make the most of our smoking time.'

They did so, and for another hour the four men sat round the fire smoking placidly, occasionally exchanging remarks, while moment by moment the hour of mystery and doom grew closer. In spite of the high degree of courage and coolness which characterised every individual who sat in that room, a certain amount of anxious expectation could not be avoided.

There was no doubt that there would be shooting. One or two men would 'lose the number of their mess'—the phrase by which among Englishmen the loss of life is generally indicated—and *who* would it be? That was the question. It was not in human nature to avoid the speculation as to whether the evil-doers would be laid low, or whether, on the contrary, one of themselves, now so instinct with life and vitality, would not be stretched lifeless upon the unpitying earth.

'Half-past eleven, gentlemen,' said the sergeant, looking at his watch. 'We must take our places, and neither move nor speak until the time comes. Mr. Newman, you had better go to bed; we will take care to have a word with them before they rouse you up. Mr. Atherstone, will you please to take that corner? Mr. Devereux, you'll stand here by me. That will give us the chance of first shot, if you care for it. Mr. Gateward, you'll plant behind that bale in the corner—out of harm's way. All you've got to think of is to light the fat-lamp we leave on the top of the wool-pack, and duck down again. They can't hurt you. Constable Gray will stop outside. As soon as he hears horses coming across the plain, he's to come in here and let us know. He's a smart young native, isn't he, Mr. Atherstone? He can track like a blackfellow, he's a pretty shot, and at riding and bush work he's a match for Billy Mossthorne or any other moonlighter that ever shook a clear skin.'

'A quiet, manly young fellow, sergeant,' said Atherstone; 'I had a talk with him coming over. You want more natives in the police to be on equal terms with these down-the-river fellows. They are pretty smart, to do them justice, and it's no use having a man who can't ride to follow them. It's like setting a collie dog after a flying forester buck.'

'We are getting some fine young men in the police now,' said the sergeant. 'There's three brothers out of one family I know, born and bred Australians; two out of the three promoted already and the other safe for it. But the time's getting close; I hope nothing's happened to the beggars.'

The sergeant's voice expressed such a pathetic tone of anxiety that the young men could not help laughing. However, all relapsed into silence shortly. The hands of the clock in the room pointed towards midnight. Would they never come? or, in a few moments more, would the deep hush of the autumn night be broken by shots and strange sounds, groans and curses?

'How the moments crawl!' said Bertram, lighting a match and looking at the brass clock on the mantel, the ticking of which sounded loud and sonorous out of all proportions to its size. 'Only a quarter-past now—it seems half an hour since I looked last.'

'It reminds me of the scene in *Old Mortality*,' said Atherstone, 'when the fanatics are waiting for the clock to strike to put Harry Merton to death. You remember one of them hears a sound in the distance which he says is "the wind among the brackens"? Another declares it to be "the rippling of the brook over the pebbles." Then a third says, "It is the galloping of horse."'

'Harry who?' asked Bertram, rather impatiently. 'I don't remember Walter Scott's characters very clearly. They all seem so devilish like one another to me.'

'Hush!' said the sergeant, in a low voice. 'By—! here they are. They'll come up fast because they know that the dogs will give the alarm. Their dart is to be in the house before any one has time to think about it.'

As the four men listened intently, a faint, dull noise in the distance gradually resolved itself into the familiar sound of hoof-beats, the measured strokes of horses ridden at speed, which came nearer and still nearer. In the stillness of the night each sound could be heard as plainly as though within the home paddock.

At this moment Constable Gray entered, his eyes glistening with excitement. 'They're near a mile off yet,' he said. 'I went to the paddock gate and listened.

There's three of 'em. Three horses, any road—that's Johnny the Pacer has joined 'em; though I don't expect *he* means fighting. The dogs'll challenge when they come a bit closer.'

'You stay outside till they dismount,' said the sergeant. 'See what door they make for, and then fall back on us. They don't know what's before them.'

The young trooper went quietly out, moving with cautious and wary tread. The roll of hoofs sounded yet closer. Suddenly there arose a chorus of furious barking and fierce growling from the pack of dogs of various breed which a head station always supports. It told that strangers—presumably hostile—had at that late hour invaded the premises.

Just then Gray re-entered. 'One man left with the horses. Two coming this way, making for the back-door.'

'It's unlatched,' said the sergeant. 'Let them come.'

CHAPTER X

In another moment steps were heard on the verandah. The growling dogs, still deeply distrustful, remained in the yard. A hand tried the back-door; it yielded, but this apparently excited no suspicion. It is not the custom to lock up houses in the bush of Australia. Burglars are unknown, and bushrangers prefer to transact their business chiefly in broad daylight—about the hour of 11 A.M. This was held to be an exceptional case.

'The storekeeper sleeps off the big room,' said some one cautiously. 'I saw him there when I was buying tobacco.'

'That's Billy's voice,' whispered Gray. 'I'd know it amongst a thousand.'

'Let's go in anyhow,' a rougher voice answered. 'There's not a dashed soul awake. Light a match and we'll have him out.'

A match flashed, lighting up the dim room, but with a result wholly unexpected by the chief actors in the melodrama. As they looked carelessly round the silent room they could hardly restrain a start of surprise as their roving eyes fell upon the sergeant in full uniform, the armed men, the levelled weapons. At the same moment Mr. Gateward arose from behind his bale, and lighting a tallow lamp, retired discreetly.

But in far less time than is occupied in tracing these ephemeral lines, thought had matured and action followed. Outmanœuvred, outnumbered as they were, the cool courage of the race was as manifest in these unhappy outlaws as in the best men of Britain's warlike forces.

'Surrender in the Queen's name!' roared the sergeant. 'It's no use, Billy; better give in quietly.'

'Not alive you don't get us,' answered the younger man, with the soft, deliberate intonation of the native-born Australian, while he raised his revolver.

The other, a grizzled, broad-shouldered ruffian, shorter than his companion by several inches, forbore reply, but firing at the sergeant's first word, shot Bertram Devereux through the body, sending also a second bullet into Harold Atherstone's right arm without loss of time. As he did so, Atherstone shifted his revolver to his left hand and fired deliberately. The robber sprang and fell on his face.

At that moment it seemed as if every firearm in the room was discharged simultaneously—the sergeant's rifle, Gray's and Mossthorne's revolvers.

When the smoke cleared, Mossthorne lay dead with a rifle bullet through his heart and with a smaller bullet through his shoulder. Bertram Devereux, bleeding profusely, was lying insensible.

Mr. Gateward had come forward from behind his entrenchment. 'Seems there was enough of you without me,' he said, 'but I felt cowardly like, stowed away behind the sheepskins. But *surely* the Doctor ain't finished this young gentleman now, as well as the poor Captain long ago?'

'By—! that rally's over quick!' exclaimed the sergeant, as he drew a full breath and gazed around, while Mr. Gateward looked on the prostrate forms with a curious mixture of relief and regret. 'Short and sharp while it lasted, wasn't it, Mr. Atherstone?' the sergeant continued, addressing himself to that gentleman, who had raised Devereux's head with his left arm, and was trying to discover the nature of the wound. 'I'd rather have taken the Doctor alive, but he gave us no time; shooting's too good for him! As for poor Billy, he's better where he is than locked up in gaol for his natural life. Now about Mr. Devereux. We must look to him first thing. He's hard hit, but it mayn't be serious. Where's Dr. Ryan? Oh! at Wannonbah. That's just right. We'll want him for the inquest besides. Constable Gray!'

The young man, who had been examining the wound in Mossthorne's breast, stood at attention. 'Take my roan horse and ride like h—l to Wannonbah. Tell Dr. Ryan to come here straight. Then go to the barracks and tell the senior constable to telegraph to the coroner straight off. Come back with him yourself.'

With a sign of assent the young man passed out into the night. A rush of flying hoofs told in marvellously short space that he was speeding on his errand on the best three-miler in the district.

'Now let's have a look at Mr. Devereux,' said Herne. 'Hold his head a little higher. How do you feel, sir? Bleeding stopped, but you've lost a lot of blood. Faintish, I daresay. Gateward, bring the brandy out of your room; a taste will do him good—and Mr. Atherstone too, for the matter of that. Seems the ball turned outward. Breathe a little, sir. That's all right,' as the wounded man took a deep inspiration. 'Take a sip of this, and we'll carry you to bed.'

'I feel better, I think,' said the wounded man, speaking with difficulty. 'I must have fainted, I suppose. That scoundrel was too quick for me. I thought he might surrender. What! are *you* winged, Atherstone?'

'Yes, worse luck,' said Harold, suppressing a groan as the broken bone grated. 'The fellow did not shoot badly, either. Billy just missed the sergeant, I see. There's his bullet mark in the door.'

'He fired first; but I didn't miss *him*,' replied that officer, with a grim smile. 'Gray's revolver bullet went through his shoulder. You dropped the Doctor in good time, Mr. Atherstone, just before he got to his third barrel. We'd better put a cloth over them now.'

As he spoke a tall white female figure appeared in the doorway. It was Pollie Devereux herself, wrapped in a dressing-gown. In her eyes, wide and shining in the half-light, was horror unspeakable, with nameless dread, as she gazed upon the forms that lay prone and so motionless.

'I *could* not wait longer after the shots ceased,' she said pleadingly. 'I was growing mad with anxiety. Mother is praying still. Are the men both dead? This one is Billy Mossthorne, I know. Poor fellow! I can't help being sorry for him. I remember his being at Maroobil.'

Her gaze, which had been for the moment riveted to the still forms which

  Lay as dead men only lie,

strayed towards the darker corner of the room, where Atherstone was supporting Bertram Devereux. The expression of her features changed instantaneously to that of agonising terror. She raised her arms with a gesture of despair, and for the moment seemed as if about to abandon herself to a transport of grief. But recovering with a strong effort of will, she sprang to the side of the wounded man, and kneeling, threw her arms around his neck, while she implored Harold to tell her if the wound was mortal.

'Oh, how his blood has been flowing!' she said. 'How pale he is! His eyes are shut. And you too, Harold? Your arm is hurt; and I was wicked enough to joke about him last night. If he dies I shall never forgive myself. Oh, my dear, dear Bertram!'

Whether this impassioned adjuration had any special effect upon the patient is uncertain, but as he opened his eyes, he smiled faintly in acknowledgment of the sympathetic words.

'Much better, dearest Pollie,' he said. 'No cause—for—alarm—much better. Flesh wound—only.' With this he turned pale and closed his eyes.

'Oh! *why* has not some one gone for the doctor?' demanded the girl passionately. 'He may die yet for want of assistance, and we are so helpless. I will go myself to Wannonbah if there is no one else.'

'Constable Gray is half-way there by this time,' said Harold calmly. 'No time has been lost. If I might suggest, you will help us best by asking Mrs. Devereux to be kind enough to have your cousin's bedroom prepared, so that we may carry him in.'

'You are quite right. Mother and I will watch by him till Dr. Ryan comes. I know I am unreasonable and foolish, but you must bear with me a little. Is your wound painful?'

'My wound is a scratch,' he answered roughly. 'Don't trouble yourself about it. Ask your mother to do what I say.' Upon this Pollie retired; and with but little loss of time Mr. Bertram Devereux was placed upon his own bed in the spacious apartment which he occupied, and with all the necessary arrangements promptly made for his benefit.

Mrs. Devereux at once devoted herself to his relief and solace as if she had been his mother. Her heart was stirred with additional tenderness as she recalled her husband's death from a similar wound at the hands of the same man. For the truth had leaked out through Mr. Gateward. The widow of Brian Devereux now knew that the hand stained with her husband's life-blood had been imbrued with that of the younger scion of the house, now wan and helpless before her; that the robber in his turn had fallen by Harold Atherstone's bullet and lay dead beneath her roof.

'Thank God! Harold is but slightly hurt,' she exclaimed. 'I regard him with a feeling I should extend to no other man as the avenger of my husband's blood. But oh! if the boy be likewise sacrificed! What a fate seems to pursue the race. May God in His infinite mercy avert it!'

Pollie had been sent to bed with peremptory commands to go to sleep instantly, and on no account to rise till she was called. The mother watched, hour after hour, with the unwearied patience of women under the excitation of grief or duty. Ere daylight broke, a trampling of horses was heard, and the man of skill, the arbiter of life and death, appeared in the chamber.

After careful examination, Dr. Ryan gave it as his decided opinion that the bullet had taken an outward course; had therefore injured no vital organ; that the faintness had been caused by loss of blood, which symptom was natural, but not necessarily dangerous. He commanded Mrs. Devereux to seek the rest she required, saying that he would take her place at the bedside of his patient. He would see what Mr. Atherstone's injury was like, and would make a search for the missing bullet in the morning.

'You will have me here for a day or two, Mrs. Devereux, so you must make me useful. It will all come to the same in the bill. I shall be wanted when the coroner comes. Fortunate escape you have all had, to be sure.'

With the morn came good tidings, and relief from the doubts and fears which had so cruelly tortured the dwellers at Corindah. Dr. Ryan, by his exercise of professional skill or the aid of exceptional good fortune, verified his favourable diagnosis by extracting the bullet, which had lodged in the outer muscle. The bleeding having ceased and the wound been dressed, there was no reason, he averred, why the patient, with such careful and intelligent nursing as he was certain to enjoy at Corindah, should not be well and hearty within the month.

The coroner too, a high and dignified official, arrived with the jury, more police, and, it appeared, likewise with a large proportion of the population of Wannonbah. The inquest was held duly and formally, a jury of twelve being impanelled, by whom a verdict of justifiable homicide was returned, the slain men being declared to have been killed in righteous defence. A rider was added to the effect that 'the conduct of Sergeant Herne and Constable Gray was deserving of high commendation, their coolness and courage rendering them, in the opinion of the jury, worthy of speedy promotion. In token of which, as well the Coroner as we the said jurors have attached our seals,' etc.

The bodies were buried in the little graveyard of Wannonbah, situated upon a yarran-shaded sandhill about a mile from that infant city. The denominational divisions, owing to the climate or other influences perhaps, were not so strictly defined as is the case in some rural Australian cemeteries, where a closely paled fence divides Protestant from Catholic, and Jew from Dissenter. At Wannonbah the dead slept much as they pleased, or rather, as their relatives desired. So Billy Mossthorne, having kinsfolk and sympathisers in the district, was buried near a maternal aunt who had nursed him in his childhood; and the Doctor, coming in for his share of indulgent forgiveness, was interred by the side of a horse-breaker of reasonably unblemished character.

Corindah was again tranquil. The inevitable sequences, great and small, of the night attack had been disposed of. The police troopers, the doctor, the coroner, the jurors had come and gone. The account *in extenso* of the 'battle, murder, and sudden death,' had been first published in the *Wannonbah Watchman*, and then had gone the round of the metropolitan and provincial papers. Sergeant Miles Herne was promoted to be sub-inspector, Constable Gray to be senior constable. Then the excitement ended, and the midnight affray at Corindah slipped into the limbo of partly forgotten facts.

One or two results, however, were not so speedily disposed of. Harold Atherstone's good right arm was of very little use to him during the ensuing half-year, the broken bones being somewhat tardy in uniting; and Bertram Devereux, through carelessness on his own part, had a relapse, and after hovering between life and death for several weeks, lay deathlike and slowly recovering in his room, needing the most careful and constant attendance to 'bring him through,' as Dr. Ryan expressed it himself. In this labour of love both mother and daughter were closely engaged for many a day after the event. It was the first time that Pollie's feminine instincts had been called into play by the necessity for personal service which a wounded soldier generally imposes upon the nearest available maiden. No situation, as persons of experience will admit, is more favourable to the development of the tender passion. The touching helplessness of the sufferer, the sense of possession and ownership, so to speak—albeit temporary—the allowable exaggeration of gratitude, the implied devotion: all these circumstances in combination render the relative positions of maiden fair and helpless knight so extremely suitable for mutual attachment, that the blind archer rarely fails to score an inner gold.

So, during the patient hours when the heavy eyes were closed, when the pale brow required bathing with *eau de Cologne*, when the spasm of pain contracted the features, when the restless fever-tossed frame lay helpless, the heart of the maiden, unfolding flower-like, grew tender and loving. She persuaded herself that a fate mightier than themselves had decreed their union. She awaited but the avowal which his eyes had long made, but which his lips had not yet confirmed, to acknowledge herself his own for ever, in life or death, here in her native land or in the unknown regions beyond the sea.

After much consideration Miss Devereux had sagely concluded that Bertram was the only man she had ever met who inspired her with feelings of sufficiently romantic intensity, who aroused in her as yet untouched heart the longing and the dread, the joy and the mystery, the strange, inexplicable, subtly compounded essence which the poets in all ages have termed love.

Why it should be so she was unable to comprehend. She told herself that he was not so strong and true as this adorer, so clever as that, or so amusing as the other; but still, why was it? Who can tell? who explain the birth of fancy, the apparition of love? But she chose to make him her hero. And if she so willed it, who was there to gainsay her?

Among the other privileges which her nursing sisterhood permitted was that of receiving and bringing in the letters of her patient. About these he had always been reticent, never encouraging conversation thereon, or admitting that any patently feminine superscriptions were not those of his mother, sisters, or cousins.

Among those which arrived by the monthly mail-steamer was one, the peculiar handwriting of which Pollie remembered having noticed at an earlier period of his sojourn. The characters were delicately formed, but the abrupt terminal strokes indicated, as she thought, no ordinary degree of determination, even obstinacy of purpose.

'Ah! my cousin Eleanor,' he said with a faint smile, as she held up the letter; 'she is my most regular, most useful correspondent. Poor little Nellie, how she would stare to see me lying here! She was my best friend when I was a graceless schoolboy, and takes an interest in the poor exile now.' He opened the other letters one by one, but did not seem to avail himself of this one. 'It will keep,' he said carelessly. 'Country news, for which I am losing my relish, poachers and pheasants, hunting and coursing, quite a journal of village historiettes.'

'A good correspondent, evidently,' said Pollie. 'Judging from the thickness of the letters, she deserves some gratitude. But when we women harness ourselves to a man's chariot, that is the treatment we chiefly receive.'

'That we are always over-indulged,' he answered, with a faint smile and a meaning look, 'I am the last man living to deny. But what must we do? It is cruel to refuse kind offices, the mere acceptance of which so gratifies the donor.'

'It may be so,' assented the girl thoughtfully, 'but the bare suspicion that my offering was *tolerated* would madden me. "All or nothing" is the Devereux motto, and it seems to embody the family temperament.'

Poor Pollie! could her eyes have pierced the inclosure!

This was the missive she unconsciously bore to the interesting sufferer:—

WYNTON HALL, *27th May* 188-

MY OWN DARLING BERTIE—You seem carelessly to have missed the last mail, at which I was woefully disappointed, and besides, I was not by any means satisfied with the tone of your last letter, sir! I read it, yes, fool that I am, over and over again, to see if I could not cheat myself into the belief that your feelings towards me were unchanged and, as mine are, unchangeable.

But I could not do it. Something, too, seems to exhale from the very lines of your writing, every letter of which I know so well, breathing coldness and change, the decay of love, the death of constancy.

Yes, Bertram Devereux, I distrust you. You are beginning to play a double game. Another woman has taken your fancy—most likely the lovely cousin of whom you wrote in your first letter, but about whom you have been suspiciously silent or guarded of late. You can deceive, have deceived many people, but you never deceived *me*. So beware! If for money, or what you men call love, you elect to play the traitor with me, to prove false to the vows which you called heaven and earth to witness, to break the compact which I have rigidly observed—*gardez-vous bien, mon ami*!

If you do not already know me sufficiently, believe this, that you will do so. I will never be deserted and scorned with impunity. I hold you bound to me by the most sacred oaths, by what I have forfeited on earth irrevocably, by what in heaven or hell I may yet have to expiate. And remember, I am capable of *anything* in the way of revenge to punish your falsehood.

If you dare to betray me, to doom me to a life of loneliness and remorse, to the torture of neglect, to the endless regret of desertion and contempt —but no, you *cannot* dream of perpetrating such fiendish cruelty. I am mad to make the accusation. My brain seems on fire. I can write no more. Believe me for ever and for ever yours only,

SYBIL DE WYNTON.

That night the sleep of the convalescent was troubled. His head moved restlessly on the pillow. His brain was feverishly active. His soothing draught failed of its effect. When Pollie came to his bedside with his breakfast she was shocked at the drawn look of his face, its pallor, and the dark rings under his eyes.

'We must keep back your home letters until you are quite strong,' she said, with an archly innocent smile, and a child's mischievous gleam in her eye, 'if they affect you like this. Your cousin's country chronicle must be strong meat for babes. But perhaps you have really had bad news, and I am talking foolishness?'

'My news is of a mixed complexion,' he said, trying to assume a cheerful expression. 'Partly good, but I have been disappointed in an important matter upon which I had set my heart. But I am so weak that the least thing tells upon me.' Here he lifted his eyes to the sympathetic, tender face, which to him now seemed as that of an angel, and a wistful appeal for pity appeared to be written on every line of his countenance.

It was the fateful moment in which heart answers to heart, and the destinies of two beings are for ever determined. It was the electric spark which fires the mine, which shatters the feeble defence raised by reason against that most ancient strategist and arch-conqueror, Love. A change passed over the girl's countenance, so swift, so subtle, so profound, that a less experienced student of woman's ways might have read the sign. To Bertram Devereux it was the plainest of print—with love's surrender in every line. He saw that pity, measureless and tender, as is woman's sympathy for man's strength laid low, had completed the spell which had been working on her sensitive, imaginative nature since his arrival. But for his wound, his near escape from death, the long hours of tendance, he doubted whether the capture of this shy, sweet wild-bird of the waste would have been effected. But now he doubted no longer. She would nestle in his bosom, would trill her song and curb her flight at his desire. The victory was won, and in the blaze of his triumph all doubts vanished as clouds at dawn. For the moment he scorned the dread which had tortured him in the dreary night-watches. He forgot that he was a coward and a traitor. He banished the thought of the sad, reproachful gaze of a forsaken woman. A new life in a new land, a new world of love and splendour lay before him.

Their eyes had met, their hands, their lips, long before this glowing, passionate thought-procession passed through his excited brain. As the girl sat by the bedside of her pale, death-stricken lover, with his wasted hand in hers, she felt as if the surrender of her every thought and feeling to his future welfare would be a price all too small to pay for the boundless happiness which had been granted to her. She was the most favoured of earth's daughters. All other thoughts and sensations showed wan and lifeless before this wondrous magic rose of love.

'But I must leave you, Bertram dear,' she said. 'You are too weak to be troubled with me. No! not another minute. Mother will bring you your medicine. You must then have a good sleep, and wake up quite a new man.' So, with one long look of tenderest denial, the fairy of his dreams vanished from the gazer's sight.

The days of Bertram Devereux's lingering in hospital were nearly ended. Over those which he still had to undergo was shed the radiance, the sweet love-light of woman's first love. He seemed to gain strength from that hour. He was soon able to lie at length and dream in the cane lounge in the shaded verandah; later on, to wander amid the orange trees by the lagoon edge, supported indeed by Pollie's fair round arm, and closely pressed to that true and tender heart. At the termination of his illness, when but for a slightly added pallor, a languor, that but accentuated his ordinary indifferent manner, no trace remained of the effects of the wound that had well-nigh proved fatal, it was then officially made known to the friends of the family that the heiress of Corindah was engaged to be married to her cousin Mr. Devereux, late of Her Majesty's Sixth Dragoon Guards.

CHAPTER XI

Even in the first flush and transport of her love-dream Pollie could not wholly divest herself of the dread that Bertram Devereux might in England have loved with all the depth of his nature some one who even now had claims upon him. In vain she asked herself why such a thought should have passed through her mind. She could not tell. But, to her deep unrest, it remained to arise and torment her at intervals, like an unquiet spirit. On the subject of his feminine correspondence she had noticed, as she thought, a departure from his usual calmness, a studied air of carelessness. What if her surmises should be true, that he was either engaged or had been the victim of one of those absorbing, soul-engrossing attachments which leave the heart of man a burnt-out volcano—barren, lifeless, dead to all succeeding influences? She would ask him. The torment of doubt on such a subject was too acute for endurance. Yet so far had she softened towards him, so far was her whole nature in a malleable state, that if he had but made frank confession she could have forgiven him.

And one day accident led up to the subject of previous attachment. Having disclaimed, on her part, the slightest tenderness in the past to living man, she looked her lover full in the face, as was her wont when aroused, and said—

'You have had my disclaimer, but tell me now, Bertram, if there lives any woman in the land you have left who is able to say, "That is my lover. This is the man whose vows, if kept, would bind him to me till death. He has broken faith and betrayed love in deserting me now." Answer me truly, on your soul's peril, and the subject shall be buried for evermore.'

As she realised in her own mind the slow torture, the melancholy days, the 'dead unhappy nights' to which a woman is doomed who waits in vain for him whom she loves, hoping against hope, refusing the sad truth, until all limit of credence be passed, so vehement an indignation fired her every feeling against the imaginary recreant that she looked like an inspired vestal denouncing the sins of a nation. 'Tell me truly, Bertram,' she said, 'that there is no hateful ghost of a dead love between you and my soul's devotion.'

A thrill passed through his inmost heart as he thought how nearly her random shaft had touched the dark secret of his life. Yet his eyes met hers fully and fairly. With men he had ever been exact and truthful, even to bluntness, but in the school of ethics in which he had been reared it was held no dishonour to lie frankly where a woman was concerned. So he bore himself accordingly.

'I scarcely think,' he said slowly, 'that a man is bound to lay bare the whole of his former life to the woman he is about to marry, nor is she wise to ask it. But,' and here he looked steadily into her innocent, trustful eyes, 'if it comforts you to think that you are the sole possessor of this invaluable heart of mine, I give you my word that no other woman has the shadow of a claim upon it.'

'I believe you,' she said; 'it removes my last lingering doubt as to our perfect happiness. In sickness, in health, in poverty or riches, by land or sea, never had man a truer mate than you will find in me.'

He drew her to his side in silence, even then repenting of his falsehood to this trusting, easily deceived creature. Still, what good would it do her to know? Why pain her sensitive heart? And was there any—the remotest—chance of his deceit being exposed? An ocean rolled between him and that passionate, headstrong woman whom he had loved with the unreflecting ardour of youth. Circumstances had certainly tended of late years to favour the idea that she would be free. In that event he had sworn a thousand times to make her his wife. But it was a contingency which might never arise. In the meantime was he to give up a career such as was now opening before him? A lovely, loving bride, who would be an envied possession wherever they went? A fortune which would enable him to satisfy all desires and tastes hitherto ungratified? Was all this to be sacrificed—for what? For a passion of which he had overrated the force and permanence in the days of inexperience? The price was too great to pay.

———————————

The marriage was fixed for the ensuing November, the first summer month. They would leave the hot plains of the North-West for New Zealand, after visiting the Australian capitals. Side by side they would revel in the glories of Rotomahana, sail on the magic lake, and marvel over the fairy terraces, returning only with the last month of autumn, when the peerless winter of the interior would be before them. A year's peaceful enjoyment of the quiet Corindah life would prepare them for the momentous, unutterably delicious expedition to the Old World, when the dream of Pollie's life would be realised and an elysium of bliss, a paradise, intellectual, social and material, would open before her.

'You romantic child!' Bertram said, looking almost pityingly at her, as in one of her imaginative flights she was, like an improvisatrice, picturing vividly a long list of pleasures to come. 'And so you believe in happiness! I only trust you will not be disillusioned when we reach this wonderful dream England of yours. And yet it may be so,' he said, smoothing her bright hair as one placates a child. 'In your company, O my sweet, I shall renew the youth I have been in danger of losing.'

Whatever might have been Mr. Bertram Devereux's secret thoughts on the subject of his prospects, he appeared to have improved outwardly, as all the neighbours and employees agreed. The alteration extended to his general demeanour. He threw off in great part the reserve which had marked his earlier tone, and assumed a genial *rôle* which no one could, when he liked, sustain better than himself. He took occasion to visit Wannonbah more frequently. He identified himself with the local interests and occupations of the district. He utilised his exceptional gifts and attainments to such purpose that all envy at his good fortune disappeared. He was finally voted by the younger squatters and the Wannonbah society generally to be a 'deuced good fellow' (when you came to know him), who would take his position among them, and be an acquisition to the district.

Harold Atherstone had gone away for change of air about the time when his arm was recovering its strength, and did not return until the engagement between Pollie and her cousin was matter of general comment. He heard of it, indeed, before he left town, at his club. What his sensations were at the announcement none ever knew. A man who bore his griefs and failures in secret, he disclosed none of his deeper feelings. When he met Pollie Devereux in her own home, it was with an untroubled brow. The kind, brave face, the wise, steadfast eyes, which she had known from childhood, were unaltered.

Pollie herself had vague misgivings that her all-important step would not meet with his approbation. Knowing that she needed not to hold herself responsible to him or any other, she yet feared lest a kind of indefinable injustice had been done by forsaking so loyal a friend. She would have felt unspeakably relieved by his full approbation and consent.

'You have heard of my engagement,' she said, as he held her hand at their first meeting after his return. 'Are you not going to give me joy and congratulate me on my happiness?'

'I may congratulate *him*' he said, a little sadly. 'My wishes for your happiness need no renewal. They do not date from to-day, as you well know. Whatever renders you happy and preserves you so will always be a part of my joy in life. May God bless you, dear, and keep you from sorrow evermore!'

In a half-unconscious way he drew the girl towards him, and kissed her as might a brother—tenderly, but without passion. Then he turned and left her, while she walked slowly and pensively towards the house. She felt that he had forgiven her; that he was too noble to harbour envy or resentment. But with woman's quickness she divined that he was grieved to the heart, and that all his self-command was needed to enable him to appear unmoved. Again and again she asked herself whether she had done wisely in following the passion-cries of her heart rather than the dictates of reason. A vain wish that she could have combined both agitated her. Of how many women and men might the same tale be told!

Mrs. Devereux was rather resigned to the arrangement as inevitable and impossible to amend than wholly approving. More acute and experienced, she had noticed the smaller defects of character in Bertram Devereux which had escaped the eye of her daughter. Not that Pollie would have suffered them to influence her. But the unconscious selfishness, the irritability, the ignoring of the tastes of others, which she had observed in her future son-in-law, did not, in her estimation, augur well for her child's happiness. When she thought of Harold Atherstone's long, unrewarded devotion, she could scarcely repress her vexation. 'What fools we women are!' she said bitterly to herself. 'We trample on pearls and gems of manhood, only to prize some glittering pebble without intrinsic value or beauty. When, as in my case, one is blessed with a husband who unites all the qualities which women love and men respect, Fate steps in and deprives her of him. How little real happiness there seems to be in this world of ours!'

While poor Mrs. Devereux thus bemoaned herself over the anomalies of life, the weeks of the short spring and early summer passed quickly along the flowery track, which, even in the Waste, is fair with wealth of leaf and blossom, with joyous birds and tempered sunshine, with high hope and joy and expectation of the coming year. The season had again been favourable. Wealth was flowing into Corindah and the neighbouring stations after the abundant fashion which, during a succession of good years, obtains in Australia Deserta. After her child was gone, Mrs. Devereux thought she would sell out and take up her abode in Europe for good. After tasting the glories and social splendours of the Old World, which she would fully appreciate, Pollie would not choose to return to Australia. Men sometimes came back to the land of spur and snaffle and wide-acred freedom, weary of cities and the artificial European life; but women, in her experience, never. They had reached across the ocean a fairy realm, where the supreme social luxuries were purchasable and abundant; servants and equipages, households and surroundings, music and the drama, art and literature, society at once congenial and aristocratic, travel and excitement—all these things were to be had for money. This they possessed. Why should they return to a land where much of this enticing catalogue did not exist, where a tithe of civilisation was difficult, the rest impossible to obtain?

So Mrs. Devereux sadly looked forward to passing the close of her days in

England—a foreign land, as far as she was concerned—far from the home, the friends, the associations of her youth, her whole life indeed, up to this stage. To her the prospect was simply one of exile and endurance.

It had been arranged that the marriage was to take place in Sydney early in November. Mrs. Devereux would go thither with her daughter immediately after that important annual ceremony, the shearing at Corindah, was concluded. The good lady preferred in a general way to manage her own affairs. She signed her own cheques, which during September and October were like the sands of the sea for multitude. Mr. Gateward was economical and loyal. Still, it was always worth while to attend to one's own business, she thought. So that, although Bertram had pleaded for an earlier day, the month of November was fixed for the wedding, principally on account of the said shearing and its responsibilities—which he had come to loathe in consequence as a comparatively trifling, but none the less vexatious, obstacle.

So when the October mail-steamer arrived he was still at Corindah, and thither his letters came. He happened to be away on the day of arrival, and Pollie, emptying on the hall table the well-filled Corindah mail-bag, sorted out the different addresses to 'Bertram Devereux, Esq., Corindah, Wannonbah, New South Wales, Australia,' as was the general superscription of his European letters. Among them Pollie descried two letters in the feminine handwriting which she had before remarked. One was addressed to her lover, one to herself.

Yes, there could be no mistake. 'Miss Devereux, Corindah, Wannonbah, New South Wales, Australia.' It was doubtless from her good, motherly cousin Eleanor, in congratulation. It was very kind of her. She had had only just time to write, too. Had the marriage been in the month of October as Bertram wished, she would have been too late.

So, with smiling eyes and unsuspicious eagerness to behold the kindly, unfamiliar lines from the probable kinswoman, Pollie opened the letter. A painter would have seized the moment for a priceless portrait, had he been at hand to mark the instantaneous changes of expression—first wild surprise, then horror; the slow, expressive alteration from trusting confidence and loving hope to disappointment unspeakable, dismay, despair.

This was the fatal sheet upon which her eyes, first flashing indignant surprise, then fell:—

WYNTON HALL, *9th August 188-.*

I should owe you an apology, Miss Devereux, for thus addressing you, would the occasion admit of unnecessary courtesy or delay. If the lifelong happiness or misery of two women—of yourself or me—be sufficient reason for disregarding ceremony, you will hold me excused, nay, bless me in the future, whatever may be the shock to your present feelings. I have accidentally discovered, what before I only surmised, that Bertram and yourself are about to be married. *He* was careful not to give me a hint of his plot—for such I must consider it to be. An Australian gentleman, a Mr. Charteris, however, happened to be staying in the house where I was visiting, and mentioned that his friend Bertram Devereux was about to be married to the beautiful heiress of Corindah. He had just heard the news from a correspondent. From what I have heard of your character, I assume that you would prefer to know the truth at all hazards. You would not be willing, as are some weak women, to pardon in the man of your choice shameless falsehood, base betrayal, and broken vows.

I swear to you now, as God shall judge me at the Great Day, that Bertram Devereux is *mine*—mine by every vow, by every tie, which can bind man to woman. Whoso accepts him, virtually takes another woman's husband with her eyes open. As events are shaping themselves I shall be shortly free. No legal obstacle to his fulfilment of the promise which he has a hundred times made, will exist. You will wonder that I choose to hold him to his bond after his proved faithlessness. May you long be free from the forbidden knowledge which would enlighten you! That I love him still is one proof more, were it needed, of the wild inconsistency of a woman's heart. I have told him of the letter to you. I fear him not; nothing earthly has power to daunt me now.

You are free to take your own course, but you are now warned against the sacrifice of your own happiness and that of the wretched and desperate woman who calls herself—

SYBIL DE WYNTON.

Holding the letter in her hand, the girl walked feebly and uncertainly, like one in a dream, to her own room. She saw through the open window a horseman riding across the plain towards the entrance gate. A few short moments since she would have flown to meet him. Now all was changed. It was the loveliest afternoon. The air was warm, yet free from the least excess of heat. A sighing breeze swept along the course of the now full-fed stream, and over the vast breadth of prairie, waving with profuse vegetation. But 'cloudless skies had lost their power to cheer.' A wintry blight had fallen upon the summer scene, banished its gladness, and turned the bright-hued landscape into a scene of desolation and despair.

Sweet love was dead. In the heart of the maiden was fixed an immovable sense of disaster—life-wreck, woe unutterable. So, when the word of doom is pronounced by the couch of those near and dear, all know that no hope or amendment, no recovery or reparation is possible for evermore.

Such was the fatal effect in the girl's mind. She had no further thought or speculation in the matter. Nothing was possible. All was at an end between them. Her life-dream was over. He had deceived her. He had betrayed and had planned to desert this other woman. In her innocent eyes it was guilt of a blackness and criminality inconceivable. All that had gone before was like an evil dream of hairbreadth escape amid avalanche and precipice, from which the sleeper starts, breathing gratitude for life and safe awakening.

She locked the door of her room, and casting herself upon the bed, 'all her o'er-laden heart gave way, and she wept and lamented.' The evening brought a partial calmness. The half-instinctive sorrow abated its poignant agony; but a dull, hopeless heartache, almost physical, remained. When the bell rang for the evening meal a maid-servant came to inquire if she had heard the summons. Her she despatched to her mother, who soon appeared with alarm and surprise in every line of her face.

'My darling, what has happened?' she exclaimed. 'Bertram and I were wondering what kept you. He has had such a pleasant day.'

'Has he read his letters?' demanded the girl, with an air of half-veiled bitterness.

'Oh, no! he said he should devote the morning to them. Most of them were family epistles, he expected, of no great consequence.'

'Oh, mother, my heart is broken! I shall die!' cried the girl, with sudden abandonment, as she threw her arms round the elder woman's neck. 'Read this, oh, mother, mother!' Here she produced the fatal letter.

As Mrs. Devereux commenced to cast her eyes over the sheet they seemed to dilate like those of one who sees suddenly an object of horror and loathing. When the end was reached she threw down the letter, as if it had been a clinging serpent, and made as though she would trample upon it.

'Let it lie there!' she said, her ordinarily serene countenance changed as the girl had seldom seen it. 'Not that I have any bitter feeling towards the miserable woman that has wrought this woe to us. No! my heart is filled with indignation against the man who has acted so deceitful, so treacherous a part, who so nearly succeeded in ruining your happiness, my darling. That you would have been unhappy, who can doubt?'

'Unhappy!' cried the girl. 'If I had come to the knowledge of his deceit, his wickedness, his cruelty in abandoning one to whom he had sworn faith, I think I should have died; all belief in truth and honour would have deserted me. I should have hated my own existence.'

'Let us thank God, my darling, that our eyes have been opened in time, ere it was too late. I never heartily approved of the affair. But Heaven knows, though I had a kind of intuitive distrust of him, I never dreamt of anything like this. And now I must give Mary her orders.'

'Oh, mother, don't leave me.'

'I will only tell her to say that neither of us will be down, that you are not well, and that I have retired for the night. She can bring up a cup of tea, which is all that either of us is likely to need.'

CHAPTER XII

When Bertram Devereux, who had waited patiently for the chatelaine's appearance, received the intimation that she would not appear again that night, that Miss Pollie being indisposed, he was requested to order in dinner, he was considerably astonished. He addressed himself mechanically to his solitary meal, but after an absent, desultory fashion and with less than his ordinary appetite. He failed to understand or account for the sudden seizure. She had walked with him to the outer gate in the morning, had patted his horse's neck, apparently as well and handsome as ever she was in her life. Why then this astonishing change for the worse? The whole thing was vexatious and disappointing in the last degree. He would go over to the barracks, smoke his cigar, and read his letters. A chat with old Gateward would be better than a solitary evening in the drawing-room.

Carrying over his mails, the young man lit a cigar and wended his way to the barrack-room. Mr. Gateward was out; the storekeeper was in the store writing up his accounts; so he threw his letters upon the large dining-room table and commenced to sort them with a strong sense of ill-treatment.

The first that attracted his notice was like the one which he had described as a cousin's to his unsuspecting *fiancée*. He opened it hastily; his brow clouded and his face grew dark as he commenced to devour rather than read the contents. 'Confound the woman!' he said with a fierce oath, before he had read half a dozen lines; 'she was born to be my ruin, I believe, and by—! she has managed it this time.'

This was her letter.

Wynton Hall, *9th August 188-.*

Bertram Devereux—When you learn that I have written by this mail to Miss Devereux explaining all, and that she has received my letter, your wrath will be bitter against me. *N'importe.* I know you as well, aye, better than you know yourself. The wound to your vanity will be sore, your spirit will chafe, nay, agonise for a time, but your ultimate good will result directly from this *éclaircissement.*

Now look me in the face, mentally, and say, what is this thing that you have been proposing to do? To marry an innocent, unsophisticated girl, partly for her beauty, partly for her money; to desert and betray me, who have loved you long, truly, wildly well; and to pretend to yourself that you were going to be happy—yes, happy! ha! ha!

No, Bertram Devereux, it is not in you. You have deceived yourself as well as her. You would have cheated me, but the attempt has failed. You *know* in your heart, or rather in your inmost consciousness, that you are incapable of love, pure, unsullied, constant—such as the poets sing of; such as this young girl, doubtless, has brought to you. In the maelstrom of London life, under the spell of old associations, you would have fallen as you have fallen before, and dragged others with you. In that hour I am the only one who has power over you. Is it not so? And my hand withdrawn from the helm, your bark and its inmates would have gone down into depths unfathomable. Angel or demon, I, and I alone, am qualified to act as your guardian. Elude my power, and you are lost, irrevocably and eternally.

I see from the papers that old Walter Devereux is dead, and has left you an income, which, though not large, ought to suffice for your reasonable needs. So take my advice once more; *soyez bon enfant*; quit the wild country of your banishment; make your adieux with the best grace you may to these Arcadian relatives; and return to a society where you have been missed—strange to say—and to a civilised life amid people that understand you. Among those who are ready to welcome the returned wanderer will most likely be your true friend as of yore,

SYBIL DE WYNTON.

He went patiently through his letters after reading this one, with a countenance which gave but little clue to the nature of the communications. One business-appearing epistle in round, legal handwriting he put aside and re-read. He then lighted a fresh cigar, and for nearly an hour remained in deep meditation before he sought his room. There he employed a portion of the night in arranging his effects, so as to be ready for that departure on the morrow upon which he had determined.

Mrs. Devereux did not appear at the breakfast table, but as he walked to and fro along the lagoon path, smoking the matutinal cigar, he saw her come into the garden. He threw down his cigar, and at once went to meet her.

She stopped a few paces ere she came to him, and looking at him with a sad, reproachful gaze, said, 'Oh, Bertram, what is this you have done to us? Did we deserve this at your hands?'

'My dearest Aunt Mary,' he said, advancing and taking her hand with a show of natural feeling which she could not resent, 'I cannot justify myself wholly, but it is due to me that I should be permitted to explain. All is over, I know, between your daughter and myself; still I do not wish her to think worse of me than is needful. When I won her love I pledged my word to her in good faith and sincerity to do all that a man might to promote her happiness. Whether I should have kept that resolution God knows, but I should have given my whole being to the task.

'By a fatal mischance she has been made acquainted with a dark chapter in my life. I do not excuse it, but it is such as many men who show fairly before the world keep locked away in secret cabinets. No doubt I deceived Pollie in denying the existence of former passages of so compromising a nature; but I thought myself justified in keeping the whole thing from her pure mind. I think so still. And now,' he said, with a return to his old charm of manner, 'I fear that nothing remains but to thank you fervently for the kindness with which you have always treated me, in sickness and in health. I owe my life to your tender nursing. Corindah will be amongst my purest, happiest memories to my life's end.'

By this time they had reached the house. Entering the old dining-room, Bertram threw himself into a chair, and Mrs. Devereux took her seat near him.

'No words can describe, Bertram,' said Mrs. Devereux, with softened air, 'how grieved I feel that we should part in this manner. I have always looked upon you as a near relative; latterly I have regarded you as a son. It is unspeakably sad to me to think that all is over—that henceforth we must be as complete strangers, as if we had never met.'

'And how little I thought yesterday that this would be my last day at Corindah!' he said half musingly. 'And yet it is best so. As if in mockery of my position, I have just been left an income by an old grand-uncle which will enable me to return to England and more or less take my former place in society.'

'I am sincerely glad for your sake,' she said warmly, 'and I know Pollie will be so also. We could not have borne that you should leave Corindah to go we knew not where. Now we shall have no fear on that score.'

'I should like to see her once before we part for ever, if you would consent,' he said pleadingly—'if it were but to hear her say that she forgives me.'

'No, Bertram!' said the matron firmly, if sorrowfully. 'Such a meeting would answer no good end. You have had forgiveness. She will never harbour a bitter thought, believe me. She has overcome her first natural feeling of resentment, such as any woman would feel who had been deceived by the man she loved. But she will grieve over the circumstances which led to your estrangement; she will pity and forgive one so near her heart as you have been.'

'If I may not see her, will you let her read a farewell letter which I will leave with you? Surely it is not necessary to debar me from the humblest felon's privilege—that of defence before condemnation.'

'She shall have your letter. I have no intention of being in the least degree harsh, Bertram, but it is by her own wish that I decline an interview. Our paths will henceforth lie separate. We shall pray for your welfare. You have a powerful will. Oh, may God guide you to use it aright! Your welfare will always concern us; but in this world we shall meet no more. And now farewell! May God bless and keep you, and forgive you even as you are forgiven by me and my poor child!'

He wrung the kindly, high-souled matron's hand in silence. An unwonted glistening in his dark eyes showed the depth to which his feelings were stirred, and if there ever was a moment in which Bertram Devereux truly repented of the sins of the past and vowed amendment of life in the future, that was the hour and the minute.

It was shortly after this interview that he held a colloquy with Mr. Gateward, and rode over to Wannonbah, with a black boy behind him, who duly led back Guardsman. He had apparently arranged for the transmission of his luggage, inasmuch as the portmanteaux, three in number, were taken on by the coach when that indispensable vehicle arrived in due course. Next morning it was announced by Mr. Gateward to the storekeeper and other employees of the station generally that Mr. Devereux had been left a fortune, which he had to go 'home' to claim, owing to law matters and other details not comprehensible by ordinary intelligence.

'He'll be back afore next shearing,' quoth one of the boundary riders. 'Leastways I know I should if I was in his place.'

'He'll be back,' replied Mr. Gateward oracularly, with an expression of countenance at once severe and impenetrable, 'when he *does* come back. If he shouldn't turn up at all, I don't know as it's any business of ours. There's as good men left behind, and would be if there were a dozen like him off by the next mail-steamer.'

Those who are of opinion that provincial gossip, along with all other British traditionary institutions, is not faithfully reproduced in British colonies, underrate the vivacious ardour of bush society when presented with a brand-new topic. No sooner was it definitely announced that Mr. Devereux had been seen on his way to the metropolis, *en route* to England, with all his portmanteaux—the same with which he had arrived—than a perfect flood of conjecture and assertion arose.

'He had come into a title and a fortune. Of course he was not going to marry in the colonies now, so he broke off his engagement at once.'

'It was Pollie's temper—nothing else—that did it; everybody knew how ungovernable that was. He couldn't stand it any longer, though Mrs. Devereux went down on her knees to him.'

'He wanted Mrs. D. to settle twenty thousand on Polly on her wedding-day, which she refused to do. He declared off at once.'

'Pollie flirted so with that Mr. Atherstone; no man could stand it. He found them walking by moonlight or something, and gave her notice at once.' 'Mr. Atherstone was in Queensland.' 'Oh, was he? Then it was some one else. It came to the same thing.'

Finally the torrent of popular criticism subsided, to settle down into a trickling rill of authentic information. It ran to the effect that Bertram Devereux had been bequeathed money by a relative, and had for some reason or other left suddenly for England.

It was neither the next day nor the next week after Bertram's departure that Pollie reappeared in her accustomed place, to lead her old life at Corindah. A weary time of illness supervened, and when the girl crept down to the drawing-room sofa to be shawled, and nursed, and petted for being graciously pleased to be better, she was but the shadow of her former self. As marked a mental change had apparently taken place, for she was mild and patient, piteously subdued in tone and bearing. How different from the wilful spoilt beauty who had turned so many heads, and who paid so little heed to good advice!

'You will have a better daughter in the time to come, mother,' she said, as she clasped the matron's neck with arms that were sadly shrunken from their former lovely roundness. 'I have had time to think over my past folly, to know who are my truest friends;' and then both wept and embraced each other, as is the way of women—the mother thankful to Heaven for the recovery of her child, the child softened by suffering and chastened by the near approach of the Death Angel.

Harold Atherstone had been far away in Northern Queensland during this eventful time. He had apparently needed stronger excitement than the everyday life of a prosperous, long-settled station; so he had elected to report upon an immense tract of country west of the 'Red Barcoo,' which, taken up by a pioneer squatter some years back, had passed into the hands of a syndicate, of which he was a shareholder.

So, from one cause or another, it fell out that Corindah seemed to be more solitary, not to say monotoned, than it had ever been before. The visitors who came were of the occasional, transitory sort; all their old friends seemed to have mysteriously vanished. The Rev. Cyril Courtenay was the only one of their *habitués* who did not fail them. He made his monthly visitation, when, indeed, Mrs. Devereux was more than usually glad to see him.

He was sympathetic in his manner, as divining that something unusual had affected his friends. With tact, as well as sincerity, he drew forth an admission of grief. This done, he essayed to lead their thoughts to the Healer of all mortal sorrow, the Bearer of burdens, the Consoler in time of trouble. He dwelt upon the unsatisfactory nature of all earthly pleasures, the disappointment inseparably connected with mere worldly aspirations, the only sure hope of forgiveness of sins, the need of repentance, the certainty of peace.

As at the time of pain and anguish, of fear and danger, the physician attains a status which in the heedless hours of health is withheld, so, in the hour of the mind's sickness, the physician of souls is welcomed and revered. Urged to lengthen his stay, the Rev. Cyril gladly consented to remain over the ensuing Sunday. His ministrations, he thought, had never been so appreciated before at Corindah. And when he quitted the locality his heart beat high with the consciousness that he had aided the consolation of the dearest friends and best supporters of the Church *in sicco*, while a yet more daring thought caused his colourless cheek to burn and his pulses to throb with unwonted speed.

The summer days grew longer and longer. The fever heat of the season waxed more and more intense. The still air grew tremulous with the quivering, ardent sun-rays. Yet no suggestion was made by Pollie to go to the sea-side or to call the ocean breezes to aid her recovered health. Her mother would have rushed off directly the great event of the year was over, but the girl would not hear of it.

'No, mother dear,' she said, 'I have sinned and suffered. I have been wilful and headstrong. Let me remain and mortify the flesh for a season. You do not mind the heat, I know, and I am strong enough now to bear it in the dear old place where I was born. We may have many a year to live here together yet, and I may as well commence to accustom myself to it.'

So the two women laid their account to remain patiently at home till the following summer, and Pollie set resolutely to work to utilise all her resources, natural and acquired. She commenced to be more methodical in the appointment of her time. She rose early and took exercise in the fresh morning air, before the sun had gained power—the truest hygienic rule in the torrid zone. She read and did needlework at appointed hours, and resolutely set herself to perfect her knowledge of French and German. She 'kept up' her music, vocal and instrumental, though it was long ere her voice recovered from a certain tremulous tendency, far different from the rich, full tones soaring upwards like the skylark to perilous altitudes unharmed. She rode regularly, or drove her mother out in the light American carriages which no station is now without. She visited the wives and children of the employees, showing a more considerate and intelligent interest in their welfare than had been before observable.

'Mother,' said the girl, as they sat together on the verandah in the waning summer-time, when a south wind speeding from the coast had unexpectedly cooled the air, 'I won't say that I was never so happy before; but I don't think I ever was so fully occupied. There is, no doubt, a sense of relief and satisfaction to be gained when one does what one can; I never thought I should feel like this again.'

'Let us have faith and patience, my darling,' said the mother, looking into her child's eyes with the measureless fondness of earlier days, 'and happiness will still come to us. Only persevere in the duties that lie nearest to you. In His own good time God will reward and bless you. After all, there are many good things in this life yet remaining.'

It was the late autumn when Harold Atherstone returned from his far, wild journeyings. A long-practised and trained bushman 'to the manner born,' he was familiar with all the exigencies of the wildest woodcraft. But from his appearance this expedition had been no child's play. Tanned and swart, almost to Indian darkness, both mother and daughter gazed at him in astonishment. He had been down with fever and ague, and was haggard and worn of aspect. He had even had a brush with the blacks, he said, on one of the far out-stations, and had managed to drop in for a spear wound. He was becoming quite a scarred veteran, he averred. However, save for a cicatrix to mark the trifling occurrence, he was unharmed. Altogether, though he had enjoyed the chances and adventures of his pioneer life, he was very glad to find himself within hail of Corindah again.

'And we are so glad to have our old Harold back, I can tell you,' said Mrs. Devereux. 'We missed him dreadfully all the summer, didn't we, Pollie? To be ill, and weak, and lonely at the same time, is hard to bear.'

Pollie made an inaudible reply to her mother's query, but as her eyes rested upon the bronzed, athletic frame, and met the frank gaze of the Australian, it may be that a comparison, not wholly to his disadvantage, passed through her mind.

'It is the first time when there was trouble at Corindah that I have been absent, I think,' he said gently. 'You must manage to have me more available in future.'

'What reason is there for your risking your life in that terrible Never Never country?' said Mrs. Devereux. 'It is not as if you needed to make any more money, or had no one to care for you.'

'One must do something with one's life,' he said simply. 'I don't know that it greatly mattered if that Myall's spear *had* gone through me, as it did through poor Williamson. I had got very tired of an easy life at Maroobil. I needed a strong change, and I got it, I must say.'

'It's positively wicked to talk in that way,' said his hostess. 'However, now you have come back, your friends must take care of you and keep you among them. You look dreadfully thin; but I suppose you're not ill, are you?' And then the kind creature looked at him with the same anxiety in her face that he remembered so well when he was a boy, over whose accidents and offences she had always mourned maternally.

'If it comes to that, it seems to me that no one looks very pink,' he returned playfully. 'Pollie's not what she used to be. You look as if you had gone through another night attack. And Bertram Devereux has gone home? What has happened? I feel abroad.'

'You are going to stay to-night, and your old room is ready for you, of course,' Mrs. Devereux answered. 'Do not allude to it when Pollie comes down. (This young lady had retired temporarily to her room.) I will tell you all about it after tea.'

Harold Atherstone looked searchingly at her, but held his peace. In a minute afterwards Pollie appeared, looking, in spite of her illness, so delicately lovely and overpowering, after his long sojourn in the desert, that all doubts and conjectures were put to flight or lost in the regained pleasure of seeing her smile of welcome and hearing the well-remembered tones of her voice.

It was a happy evening. Apart from 'love and love's sharp woe' there *is* such a thing as friendship, pure and unalloyed, between people of differing sexes. The sentiment of these friends was deep and sincere—founded upon sympathy, congenial tasks, and the long experience of mutual truth, loyalty, and affection. They were honestly glad to see each other again. Love temporarily divides friends, and, as it were, elbows out all other claimants. But as its fervour declines, the purer flame burns with a deeper glow. As the years advance, the fires of passion wax dim; the altar reared to friendship regains its votaries; while the more ornate and ephemeral edifice is too often deserted, empty, and ungarnished.

Thus, at their pleasant evening meal, all was mirthful interchange of news and adventures since last the little party had met. Harold's favourite wine of the remembered brand was brought out as of old; then Pollie was persuaded to sing some of her oldest songs, while Mrs. Devereux and their guest talked confidentially in the verandah. It seemed as if the happy old Corindah days had come again, when no malign influence intervened; when, in Mrs. Devereux's eyes, all things were peacefully tending towards the cherished aspiration of her life. Finally, when the parting hour—later than usual— arrived, each secretly confessed to a sensation so nearly akin to the joy long since departed from their lives, that not only wonder but even a *soupçon* of hope was commingled with its formation.

Harold Atherstone had been placed fully in possession of facts by Mrs. Devereux, as they sat on the verandah in the hushed southern night, while Pollie's sweet voice trilled nightingale-like through the odorous breath of the rose and the orange bloom. He heard how she had been deceived, wounded in her tenderest feelings, and was now deserted and left desolate. When he thought of her lying wearily on a bed of sickness, wan and wasted, heart-sore and despairing, he could not repress a malediction upon the head of the man who had received such unstinted kindness at the hands of the speaker, and had thus repaid it.

When the tale was finished he took her hand and pressed it silently. 'The poor child has suffered deeply,' he said; 'but matters are best as they are. Who knows but that deeper, more irrevocable misery might have been her lot had she not been warned in time? I mourn over the change in her, but she is returning to her old ways, and the memory of her sorrow will become yet more faint. Her youth and pride, with the resources at her command, will enable her to divest herself of all trace of what was one of the inevitable mistakes of youth.'

'You think then that she acted rightly in refusing to see him again?'

'Unquestionably; no other course was possible. I never thought him worthy of her. But he was her choice, and as a man of honour I could not disparage him, even had I any other grounds than those of mere taste and prejudice, which I had not. The event has proved that my instinctive distrust was correct. I need not tell you how I rejoice that she is again free and unfettered.'

He said no more. The summer had passed. The nights became longer, colder. The calm, peaceful, autumnal season, which in this south land brings no fall of the leaf, commenced to herald the mild but well-marked winter of the plains. It was the Indian summer of their old, peaceful Corindah life. They rode, and walked, and drove together, the three friends, much as in the old days before the advent of the disturbing stranger from beyond the sea. Then Harold Atherstone had been the favourite companion of the girl, the trusted friend and counsellor of the elder woman. The *bon vieux temps* had returned. Once more the heavens were bright, and the storm-cloud had disappeared with the tempest which had so nearly wrecked the frail bark of a woman's happiness.

And yet both were changed. The girl, mild and pensive, was almost humble in mien. All her wilfulness and obstinacy had departed. A deeper, more reasoning spirit of advance and inquiry seemed to possess her, to mould her every action and thought. He, on the other hand, had acquired broader views of life, and had seriously modified many of his earlier opinions.

But their parting was near. Harold received a telegram, without warning or notice, which necessitated instant action. His presence was again required at the far North, where everything was going on as badly as could be imagined. The chief manager lay dying of fever, the blacks were troublesome, and becoming emboldened, had commenced to scatter off the cattle. To mend matters, a drought of unprecedented severity had set in. 'If Mr. Atherstone did not go out,' the telegram stated, 'the whole enterprise might be wrecked, and ruinous loss accrue to shareholders.'

At first he rebelled, swore stoutly, indeed, that he would not go. He would let things take their course. He was happy where he was, and there was no reason why he should risk his life and tempt again the dangers of the Waste. However, cooler reflection decided him to take the field as a duty to his comrades in the enterprise, as well as to the shareholders, who had risked their money perhaps on the guarantee of his known judgment and reputation for management.

He made his preparations quickly, as was his wont, bade farewell to Corindah and its inmates, and set off on the long, hazardous journey.

Somehow Corindah seemed more lonely than ever. He had been very kind and thoughtful as a brother, but no word of warmer admiration had passed his lips. Pollie pursued her tasks and occupations with accustomed regularity, but was more unequal in her spirits than ever. One day her mother surprised her in tears. A letter had been received from Harold, and the tone of it had aroused her from habitual indifferentism.

'Why is he always so studiously cool and brotherly?' she said, with something of her old impetuosity. 'Does he think that I am likely to misconstrue his feelings? That he requires to keep a guard over his expressions? But I know how it is. He has met some one else in that far country. He spoke of some English families settled there. I have lost his love, which once was so truly mine. I despised it then. Now I am rightly punished by contempt and desertion.'

Mrs. Devereux gained from this little speech a fresh and accurate insight into the state of her daughter's heart. It went to confirm the suspicion which she had lately entertained that the recent companionship of Harold Atherstone, the daily experience of his strong, true character, had not been without its effect. He had come most opportunely to cheer their loneliness. His manner had somewhat altered, too, of late, they had remarked; had become more gay and carelessly mirthful, more easy and conventional. His travels and adventures had supplied him with a larger field of observation, had added to his conversational powers, or else he had exerted himself exceptionally for their entertainment.

His sense of humour seemed to have developed, and withal there were occasional touches of tenderness and deep feeling which, always latent, had been rarely exhibited. Both women confessed that they had never done justice to the versatile force of his character; never had they dreamed he could exert fascination in addition to his power of compelling respect.

And now he was gone thousands of miles away—the true friend, the gallant gentleman, the loyal lover—to brave the risks of the Waste, perhaps die there, as had done many a brave man before him; perhaps to be attracted by some newer, fresher face, never to return to his old allegiance. The thought was bitter. No wonder that Pollie's tears flowed fast.

Harold Atherstone had exhibited his habitual self-control in quitting Corindah for a long absence without making sign or giving expression to his feelings. He had carefully considered the situation, had come to certain conclusions, had decided upon his course of action. His feelings were unchanged with respect to Pollie. It had been hard to bear, almost unendurably torturing, to know that she preferred another; to witness her bright glances and hear her tender tones directed towards one whom in his heart he deemed unworthy of her. In his chivalric generosity he felt this to be the crowning bitterness of the whole. Unable to bear it longer, he elected to join this dangerous enterprise, reckless of life and health, hoping only for 'surcease of sorrow' in peril and privation.

But on his return he found that the enchanted portal had been opened, the captive princess liberated. The glamour had fallen from her eyes. The magic fetters had been unloosed. He could picture the scorn and indignation with which she had renounced Bertram Devereux for ever. From his lifelong knowledge of her character he believed that she had freed herself from the memory of his treason as from something foul and revolting; that it had fallen from her pure soul as earth from a golden robe; that she had returned instinctively to the simple loyalty and freedom of her youth. From his experience of life and woman's nature he foresaw that she would turn to him as to one of the lost ideals of her girlhood, if only he were not precipitate and premature. These were not the faults with which men charged Harold Atherstone. So he returned silent and self-contained to the far North.

His unswerving courage and iron will stood him in good stead in this supreme hazard.

When Harold returned from the far country, his friends at Corindah were unaffectedly glad to see him. Pollie especially was so radiant in renewed health and beauty that he felt irresistibly impelled to ask the momentous question.

He chose an appropriate time and place—one of the star-bright, cloudless nights which in the southern hemisphere so glorify the majestic solitude of nature. Low-toned and musical was the whispering breeze which, stealing over the 'lone Chorasmian waste,' stirred the slumbering lemon sprays and murmured to the love-fraught roses as they walked by the margin of the lakelet, all silver-bright in the wondrous transparent atmosphere. It seemed as though, after the rude experiences of his desert life, he had re-entered paradise. He was so delighted to return, so charmed with the warm welcome accorded to him, that he would never more return to the wilderness. He would indeed promise and guarantee to do so, but on one condition only. Need we say what that was, or that the concession was made?

'Are you sure that you think me worthy of your love, after all my folly?' murmured she. 'But I have suffered—you will know how much. I have repented, and, dearest Harold, I will try to be the woman you would have me to be.'

'There has been but one woman in the world for me,' he said, clasping her to his heart. 'She is mine now for ever; life holds no other prize henceforth that I will stretch out my hand to seize.'

What more remains to tell? Pollie's probation was ended. Her wayward, errant woman's heart, 'with feelings and fancies like birds on the wing,' had found rest, relief, and safety on the manly breast of Harold Atherstone. Henceforth there was no fear, uncertainty or anxiety. She felt a wavering dread at times lest he, requiring so much love (as she had gauged his temperament), would find her nature unequal to the demand. But, as generally happens in similar cases, this proved to be a groundless apprehension.

As for Mrs. Devereux, she was prepared to sing 'Nunc dimittis.' Her cherished hope had been realised. Maroobil and Corindah in conjunction would make a princely property, no matter how many there might be to inherit it. In every relation of life Harold was a tower of strength. Now she had a son whom she had loved since the days of his fearless childhood. Now was she proud, happy, thankful. Providence *did* sometimes settle affairs of mortals aright. She had only to thank God humbly on her bended knees that night, to pray with tears and sobs for her darling's happiness, believing in her inmost heart that it was now assured and lasting.

And she was happy—perfectly, utterly, completely, if there be such a thing in this world below. They lived for the greater part of the year at Maroobil or

141

Corindah, choosing by preference the quiet home life, where they had full enjoyment of each other's society, varied only by the ordinary demands upon their hospitality, which they were careful to recognise fully as of old. Maroobil was voted to be the pleasantest visiting-place in the West, and Mrs. Harold Atherstone the most perfect hostess.

'What a fortunate thing that you were able to sell out of that horrid Queensland country so advantageously!' said Mrs. Atherstone a month after their marriage, when, resting under the shadows of Mount Wellington, they absorbed rather than admired the charms of the varied Tasmanian landscape. 'I shall never forget my fears on your account during that last journey.'

'I take great credit for not committing myself before I started,' he said. 'It grieved me sore, but I held out. I was mortally afraid, too, that you might have another proposal in my absence. I suppose you hadn't?'

'Well, not quite a proposal, only from Mr.——.'

'Why, you insatiable woman, you don't mean to say that? Tell me this moment who it was. Why didn't I know before?'

'Don't look so fierce, and I'll confess everything. It is not much. But Mr. Courtenay, the Rev. Cyril, *did* call while you were away.'

'Confound him! The smooth-faced humbug!' growled Harold, twirling his moustache. 'However, "Better men than he," etc. Well, go on, Circe——'

'None of your heathen innuendoes, or I stop. But really, love, the poor fellow said he had been left a competence by an uncle, and that as he could not now be accused of mercenary feelings, he wished me to know, etc.; we should be able to do so much good with his means and those Providence had gifted me with. Of course I explained gently that it could not be. I felt quite clever, I assure you. I had only to alter what I said to Mr. MacCallum a very little. It would have served you right, sir, if I had taken him after your leaving me in that way.'

'H—m, you won't be left much in future, madam, as you are not to be trusted.'

Brian Devereux Atherstone and Harold the second were respectively three years and one year old when, the season being a good one, and wool above the average, it was decided by the collective wisdom of the family that a suitable opportunity had occurred for the long-promised visit to Europe. Mrs. Devereux had no objection to offer, except that the dear children might not in all respects be benefited. But this was overruled. Statistics were quoted to the effect that on board the P. and O. and Messageries steamers children were stronger, happier, and longer lived than on shore. Finally the project was carried out, Mr. Gateward being left in full possession of the station for the three years which it was intended that the tour should embrace.

Why attempt to portray here with what supreme, almost unutterable, delight two cultured persons of congenial tastes and fresh, unworn mental palates savoured the intellectual banquets placed before them? Again and again did Mrs. Atherstone declare that her cup of happiness was filled to the brim, even running over.

On one of those elysian days, as Pollie sat dreamily under the columns of the Temple of Poseidon, while around them stretched the green plain of Pæstum, Harold, who had been reading Galignani with a Briton's never-failing interest, handed the paper to her with a pencil-marked paragraph.

Her cheek paled for an instant, then glowed more brightly, her eye flashed, her head was raised, as she ran over the following extract from a society paper:—'We observe with regret that the demise of Sir Ralph de Wynton at his seat, Wynton Hall, Herefordshire, took place on Thursday last. The announcement will not surprise many who were acquainted with the sombre family history of the last male heir of this ancient race. The deceased baronet had been for many years a hopeless invalid. It was believed, indeed, that he was placed in confinement at those periods when he was supposed to be travelling abroad. Owing to differences which had arisen at an early period of their union, it was generally supposed that Lady de Wynton, who resided chiefly at Florence, had arranged a virtual separation. The estates, with all property, real and personal, excepting only her ladyship's ample jointure, pass to Colonel de Wynton of the Life Guards.'

'So, poor thing, she has been freed from her fetters at last!' said the fair reader, as she handed back the paper with a smile of loving content and absolute trust to her husband. 'She will now be free to marry Bertram, and I trust sincerely they will be happy. I always pitied her from my heart, and thought it a case of cruel wrong and injustice.'

'H—m!' replied Harold, with cautious non-committal. 'I suppose very probable. "More sinned against," etc. But I don't wonder at your sympathy. You are under greater obligations to Sybil, Lady de Wynton, than to any living woman, the grandmum only excepted.'

'Obligations indeed! Why?' she demands, in much astonishment. 'Oh! I know —though it's like your cool audacity to say so—because but for her I should have gone through the wood, and through the wood, and taken—as I fully believe and acknowledge *now*—"The Crooked Stick" at last.'

THE END